Mountain Man Daddy Series

Mountain Man Handyman (Book 4)

S.E. Riley

The Redherring Publishing House

Mountain Man Handyman (Book 4)

Table of Contents

Prologue

Della

"I can't do this anymore," I whispered, my eyes wet. I looked at Greer, his expression marred by a frown. He was just as upset. I could see it in the redness rimming his eyes. He was angry, too, and I couldn't really blame him.

"Do what?" he asked, throwing his arms up in defeat. "Be with me?"

It'd been a year since his parents died, and while I helped him through it as best I could, I could no longer pretend I was happy. But he wouldn't understand. He already thought my decision had something to do with him when it didn't. Not really.

I licked my lips. They were wet and salty from my tears. I was trying my hardest to stem them, not when it felt like my heart was shattering inside my chest. I attempted to inhale a full breath, but I couldn't manage that either.

Greer pulled his hand through his hair, visibly confused and frustrated, and I couldn't, in any way, blame him for how he was feeling.

"I need more, Greer. This..." I waved my hand around my grandmother's cabin, "...isn't enough anymore." Nanna's cabin was a metaphor, though, for Kipsty Little Town itself, the small town we called home.

Greer expelled an angry sigh, looking between me and my

luggage. I was planning on leaving before he came home, which I realized may have been cowardly, but I wanted to spare us this pain. I didn't have the courage to face Greer before I left, and had written him a note instead, but he surprised me by coming home early for the weekend. He was studying Landscape Architecture at Colorado University and could only manage to come home on a Friday afternoon and stay for the weekend. It was another reason I couldn't keep doing this and why I needed to leave. He was at school all week, and it felt as though all I really did was wait for him to come so we could spend a morsel of time together.

"Is it me?" he asked. His voice cracked, making me feel worse than I already did. I wasn't only breaking my 18-year-old heart. I was breaking his too. And as much as it killed me, I couldn't keep lying to myself anymore.

Kipsty Little Town had become too small.

I'd lived here my whole life, and all I'd ever really wanted was to leave and find something bigger. And, to some degree, something better, I guess. I felt trapped here, stuck on a hamster wheel that kept spinning without going anywhere. If I tried to explain to Greer the restlessness that had resided under my skin, and in my veins, for the last year, he wouldn't understand.

I took a step toward him, and he matched it by taking a step away from me. The physical distance between us hurt. I loved him with every part of me, but our emotional distance was fraught with tightly bound tension on the verge of snapping us in two. And that, I realized, was what hurt the most. I had loved this boy from the time I was fifteen, he'd been my first everything, and it brought me no pleasure at all to inflict any kind of hurt on him.

But three years later, I had to do what was best for me, and this town, staying here, was not it. But Greer wasn't listening to me. This had almost nothing to do with him, yet in his eyes, I was leaving because of him. That couldn't be further from the cold, hard truth.

"It's not about you," I replied, swiping at the tears sliding down my cheeks. I had to find a way to pull myself together and stay strong in my own conviction. "I love you," I told him fervently. "I'm in love with you. But I can't stay here, Greer. I'm unhappy, and I'm not like you. I can't see my future in this godforsaken podunk town. I want more for my life than being stuck here and living the same life my grandmother has lived."

My life in Kipsty wasn't bad. It had never been. I was raised by a very strong woman who profoundly influenced the woman I'd become. And as much as it hurt my grandmother to see me leave, she understood, better than anyone, why I was doing it. My mother did the same thing when she was my age, except she showed up back here a year later with me in tow and dropped me off on my grandmother's porch. She never stuck around after that. And as much as I hated to admit it, the same restiveness that filled her spirit, existed in me, and it was about the only thing she gave me, besides my blonde hair, blue eyes, and curvy build.

Greer winced, and I watched him withdraw from me. It was like experiencing the loss of air in your lungs. And I was cold without him. Chilled to my marrow. He unknowingly took my air and heat and stepped away. The withdrawal was acute, and I felt it in every cell in my body. But I wouldn't cave. I wouldn't change my mind, and I think he was starting to realize that.

"Then I guess there's not much left for me to say," he told me quietly. For the briefest moment, he closed the gaping space between us, held my head between his strong and steady hands, kissed my forehead, and inhaled my scent one last time. I reveled in that affection, knowing it would most likely be the last.

"I hope you find what you're looking for, Del. I really do."

He stepped back and gave me one last look, his green eyes red and filled with so much I couldn't quite put a name to. He shook his head and walked towards the front door of the cabin I'd lived in my whole life. It was filled to the brim with memories. Memories I'd also have to leave behind once I was gone. It wouldn't serve me to hold on to anything if I wanted to move forward. The memories I'd keep were those of Nanna and me because they'd get me through the hard times ahead.

Greer glanced at me from over his shoulder and opened his mouth as if he had something else to say, but instead, he walked out and shut the door. I collapsed against the back of the sofa, and a sob escaped from between my lips. I slapped my hand over my mouth to smother the sound, but it was difficult when it felt like my lungs weren't working.

The pain in my chest intensified, and I looked up just in time to see my grandmother, Delia, stop between the living room and the kitchen. Without uttering a word, she opened her arms, and I rushed to her, seeking the kind of comfort only she could give me.

"I think I broke my own heart, Nanna," I cried, my head on her shoulder. She wrapped her arms around me, rubbing her hand over my back. "He'll never forgive me."

"Hush now," she replied. "You knew this was the hard part, Della." She pushed me back, hands on my shoulders. "You know in your heart of hearts that you won't be happy if you stay, and you'll only end up resenting that boy if you stay for him. You understand, baby girl?"

I nodded and swallowed the knot of tangled emotions clogging my throat. "Leaving you is hard, too," I told her. And it was. She raised me, gave me a beautiful life, and made sure I turned out to be a decent human being. Everyone in town loved her, but I was so damn lucky she was my family. I was who I was because she made me.

"I know," she replied gently. "But I want you to be happy, Della. You've been a dreamer your whole life, and I'd never stand in the way of those big dreams just to keep you here with me." Her eyes glossed over, and she sniffled. "I love you more than life itself, Della Marie, and I'm so proud of who you are." She dropped a kiss on my cheek. "The bus will be here soon," she reminded me. "Promise me you'll call when you get there, okay?"

"I promise." I threw my arms around her delicate frame and

held her close, breathing in the scent of cinnamon and sugar. "I love you."

"I love you more," she whispered. We parted, and she helped me carry my luggage to the car before she drove me to the bus stop outside town. I didn't look back when I boarded that bus.

I wish I had.

Chapter 1

Della

Mid-December, 11 years later

I shivered next to my car and held my phone up in an attempt to get some decent cell reception. But I was in the Colorado mountains, and it was snowing. The flurry of white snowflakes whirled around me, and I glanced at my car. I was driving up the mountain when I swerved for a squirrel, *a squirrel*, and now my poor Lexus was in a ditch on the edge of a curve in the road.

Sigh.

You'd think a Lexus SUV could handle a wet road and some snow, but it turns out that even the flashiest of vehicles eventually succumbed to bad weather. The worst part was there was no traffic on this road, not this deep into the mountains. I huffed out a frustrated breath, the hot air coming out in a puff. There was little I could do at this point except hope that someone would be coming up this road.

I tried getting my car out of the ditch, but the wheels spun on the wet ground, making it worse. I was capable in many ways but getting a car out of a ditch was beyond what I could do. I climbed back into my car, holding my useless phone in my hands as I tried to stay warm. I didn't want to leave the car idling for long, so I'd turned the ignition off an hour ago. My only option was to wait.

My head hit the headrest, and I squeezed my eyes closed. It was a freak accident, but it was easy to assume it would only happen to me because I was making my way to my hometown after eleven years. Though I was here just over a year ago for Nanna's funeral, but I didn't stay long. And now her cabin was mine. Along with the diner she owned on Main Street.

The whirr of an engine rose above the sound of the wind, and when I glanced in my rearview mirror, I saw a navy-blue Ford Ranger pickup truck rounding the corner. I scrambled to get out of my car and wave down whoever was driving. I couldn't see a face through the falling snow, but I needed help, and this was the first vehicle I'd seen since my car enthusiastically went nose-first into the ditch.

The pickup slowed to stop in front of me, and I exhaled a breath of relief. I waited for the driver to climb out, and I sucked in a breath when he did—shock black hair, muscular build, and brown eyes with sharp brows when he faced me.

"Della Marie, is that you?" he asked, the pitch of his voice high.

"Kyle?" I asked, brows furrowed. "You know I don't like being called that."

"Well I'll be damned," he murmured under his breath. "Same old sass, I see." He walked closer and surprised me when he picked me up and spun me around. I surprised myself when a laugh broke free from between my lips. He put me down and looked me up and down.

"Damn, you look good," he remarked, his lips tilted in a friendly smile. My lips were stiff, but I did my best to return it. He was my first blast from the past, yet another person I'd hurt the day I left. He was Greer's best friend, but we were just as close growing up seeing as we were in the same age group. He'd since grown into his muscular build and had that whole lumberjack thing going on.

He glanced between me and my car. "You need some help?"

"I, uh, got myself stuck in a ditch," I replied. "Forgot how tricky this stretch of road can be."

When he took a proper look at my car, he whistled. "With a car like that, you shouldn't have a hard time on these roads." I was too embarrassed to explain how I landed myself in this situation, so I didn't.

"Think you can get me out?" I asked instead. He scratched the side of his face and blew out a breath while checking my car. "Doesn't look like there's any damage, but I don't have a tow kit in my car. You headed into Kipsty?"

Like I'd be going anywhere else if I was on this damn road.

"Yeah." I sighed. "I've been stuck here for an hour, though. You're the first person I've seen."

"Well..." he looked between me and my car again, "...I can take you into town myself, and come back for your car. That work for you?" I knew the chances of my car being stolen around here were next to nil, but I was still hesitant. However, I was wholly aware that I had no other choice.

"If you won't mind, I'd appreciate it."

Kyle nodded once, and I popped open the back of my car. He looked at my luggage with raised brows. "You moving back or something?"

"Or something," I muttered under my breath.

He chuckled. "I know a whole lot of people who will be surprised to see you, Della. That's for sure."

Rather than respond—I didn't want to think about how *anyone* was going to react when they saw me pull in—I started lifting my suitcases out of my car and wheeling them over to Kyle's pickup. Between the two of us, it took about ten minutes. I grabbed my purse and locked my car before climbing into the passenger side of Kyle's pickup. He turned the key and drove back onto the slick roads. Unlike me, Kyle had chains on his tires, dramatically improving his grip on snow-covered tar.

Not one to sit in silence, Kyle gave me a sidelong look. "So, you never answered my question. You moving back to Kipsty or what?"

There was no getting around this. I blew out a hard breath. "Yeah," I replied quietly. "I'm taking Nanna's cabin."

He chortled and shook his head. "Never thought I'd see the day that you would come back to Kipsty Little Town. And for good, too." I didn't bother correcting his assumption about how long I'd be staying. I was still deciding.

After my life in New York fell apart at the seams, I just needed a place I could run away to, and Nanna's cabin seemed an obvious choice.

"We've all been waiting for a *for sale* sign to pop up," Kyle continued. I looked at his profile, noting how much he had changed. But I supposed time does that to all of us. Life experience too. We all had to grow up eventually. "Most of us were sure you'd sell it."

The thought of selling Nanna's cabin had a band tightening around my chest. I may have left Kipsty when I was eighteen with no intention of ever coming back, but, "I'd never *ever* sell Nanna's cabin." Which was now *my* cabin.

He huffed out a laugh. "You might feel differently when you see it."

"What does that mean?"

Kyle rested his elbow on the door and looked over. "We've had a few nasty storms over the past few weeks. Last I checked, Nanna Delia's cabin had a tree fall on the roof, and you now have a hole in the living room. Not sure you'd actually be able to stay there until it's fixed." My heart plummeted into my stomach.

"Is it bad?" I asked, a lilt to my voice that sounded a whole lot like panic. I had no one in town who could have let me know in advance about the state of the cabin. "Can I stay at the inn?" I asked. The last time I was in town, the inn was still there.

Kyle shook his head just as we rounded another bend and turned left onto the road that led straight into Kipsty. "Inn's full," he replied. "Wedding party, I think."

It wasn't unheard of to have weddings here. It was actually

quite beautiful, especially for a winter wedding. I fiddled with my fingers, partly because I was worried about where I was going to stay. I was suddenly nervous being back here after so long.

Kyle drove down Main Street and headed towards the cabins. He stopped his truck outside mine and climbed out to help with my luggage. While he unloaded my suitcases, I walked up the porch steps and yelped when the wood beneath my feet gave way. I slipped and fell on my ass, my foot stuck between where the wood had splintered. Kyle rushed over and helped me stand.

"You okay?" I rotated my ankle and gave him a nod.

"Fine," I sighed. "You weren't kidding about the state of this place."

I unlocked the front door, and the faint smell of pine, cinnamon, and sugar tickled my nose. Even though it had been over a year since my grandmother had passed away, it still smelled like her. "You weren't kidding about the roof," I murmured under my breath.

Kyle walked in, wheeling my suitcases in behind him, and stopped next to me. "We've been trying to fix all the cabins that the storms have hit, but it's a lot for just me and..." He stopped talking and cleared his throat, rubbing the back of his neck.

"You and?" I prodded.

His expression was reticent, as if he didn't want to say more. I stared at him expectantly. "Say it, Kyle, how bad could—"

"Me and Greer," he interrupted, his expression changing to one of concern. My heart flopped around at the sound of his name, and I had to admit that the other reason I was nervous about coming back was seeing Greer.

"We run a small construction company together," he explained, and I lifted my hand.

"It's okay, Kyle. No explanation needed." Kyle was Greer's best friend, had been since they were in diapers, and it was inevitable that I'd not only hear about Greer but see him too. I just wasn't ready for the latter. My phone started going off in my purse now that I had reception, and when I saw it was my ex, Alex, I sent it to voicemail. He'd been trying to reach me for hours, but I had little doubt that what he had to say wasn't all that important. I had something bigger to worry about, like where I was going to stay.

"You sure the inn is full?" I asked, turning around. The hole in the roof was substantial, and with the wind came the snow and other debris. It was uninhabitable. Which meant I was basically homeless. Just what I needed.

"I can call my mom and confirm," Kyle replied. "But when I spoke to her this morning, she was already complaining about having her hands full with the guests."

I exhaled a heavy breath, hands on my hips. "Then I'll just have to make it work," I told him. "Thanks for your help. You'll, uh, let me know what I owe you for towing my car?"

He gave me a look and dryly replied, "I'm not making you pay shit, Della. I'll go fetch your car now and leave it out front for you."

I thanked him, handing him my keys, and only once he'd left did I fall onto the old, worn sofa. Dust puffed up around me, and I sneezed. Obviously, the place needed some work, but perhaps if I could fix it up, piece by piece, I could fix myself up the same way.

Chapter 2

Della

Kyle towed my car to the driveway less than an hour later, finding me in the same spot I had slumped into. My mind had been consumed with where to start to make the cabin a little livable. He handed me the car keys, reassuring me that the car was fine before confirming that he had called his mother and the inn was full for the next week. He only left minutes later after asking if I was sure about staying in the cabin. I stood by the door and watched him drive away before I quickly kicked into action. I couldn't stay idle for long.

I went into the kitchen, looking for a broom and dustpan. They were exactly where Nanna had left them. I started in the bedrooms, moving around the debris in the living room. There were only two rooms and a small bathroom. Nanna had one of the smaller cabins. The larger two-story cabins were a row up from here. I wasn't surprised to see that my childhood bedroom had stayed the same. The small double bed was pushed against the far wall, and beside the door stood a simple white dresser covered in glitter stickers from when I was younger. In the corner stood the small closet that once kept all my clothes, most of which came from Goodwill in town.

I removed all the bedding and changed it, swept the floor as best I could, and then moved on to Nanna's room. It was slightly bigger than mine, and I would probably take it now that the cabin belonged to me.

I was halfway through mopping the floors—and ignoring the growl in my stomach—when there was a knock on the front door. I rested the mop against the wall and opened it, not entirely prepared for who I'd see. It could have been anyone, really.

People in Kipsty were nosey, and I was sure the town would be abuzz with news of my arrival soon enough—if it wasn't already. It was possibly the only thing I wasn't looking forward to.

Greer stood tall and imposing on my porch, having grown into his muscular form. His blonde hair was messy, and his green eyes clouded over beneath sharp brows. His jaw was sharp, like his cheekbones, and his lips were full and round. I sucked in a hard breath. Okay, maybe seeing Greer was something else I wasn't looking forward to, and now he was here, dressed in dark denim, work boots, a flannel shirt, and a black hooded jacket.

He's really embraced the whole mountain man vibe.

"Greer." His name left my mouth on an exhale.

"I didn't believe Kyle…" he said, his tone hard, "…when he said you're back."

My throat worked as I tried to swallow, but it was no use. It felt as though someone had stuffed a wooly sock in my mouth.

"What are you doing here?" He barked. I flinched at how harshly he'd posed such a simple question. I blinked and remembered myself. We weren't kids anymore, and he didn't get to speak to me like my arrival was inconvenient. I straightened my spine, swallowed around the emotion in my throat, and met his gaze.

"I'm moving in," I said, keeping my tone firm but conversational. It wouldn't do me any good to meet his confrontational countenance with the same.

"You hate Kipsty," he stated, unabashed by his own lack of diplomacy.

I cocked my head and *really* looked at him. At how he'd changed. He was no longer a boy but a 30-year-old man. An attractive one at that. Then again, he was always attractive to me. He *was* my first love. And I never did see him when I came back for Nanna's funeral. I didn't look very hard, though. I was grieving the only family I had left, and Greer was the last person on my mind that day.

"Thanks for the reminder." I huffed. "You come here for a reason other than to confirm that I'm really here?"

He licked his top lip, resting his hands on his hips. Even his stance was hostile and imposing. And for what? Because I dared show my face in my hometown? That wasn't going to fly with me. I had every right to be here, whether he liked it or not. "Was it to ask why I'm here?" I guessed.

He gritted his teeth, a muscle popping in his angular jaw, and like a pro, he evaded my question with one of his own. "Kyle tell you you can't stay here?"

I looked behind me and tried to hide my grimace. When I faced him again, I smoothed my expression. "The rooms aren't damaged," I told him. "It's just the living room."

I stumbled back when Greer stepped forward and into my personal space. He was taller than I remembered. And a whole lot bigger, too. Menacing. He eyed the hole in the roof and the mess on the floor.

"You can't stay here," he said, his voice low. "You'll freeze or worse, Della." It was the first time since he'd shown up that he'd bothered to say my name, and hearing it from his mouth made my skin shiver and my bones shake. He didn't say it with any kind of reverence. In fact, he said it with irritation lacing his tone. But in that deep timbre of his voice, I still felt it down to my toes, which curled in my boots. The truth is, he was right, but on principle alone, I wasn't about to allow him to tell me what I could or couldn't do.

"Pretty sure I'll be just fine, *Greer*. Besides, where am I supposed to stay? Kyle said the inn is full."

"Your car is a better option than this," he replied, jutting a thumb back towards my truck. "You know you'll freeze your ass off in here. It's as cold as a witch's tit outside, and the snowfall is just getting worse. Thought you'd remember what the seasons were like here." His dig was subtle, but I felt it nonetheless.

"I'm not sleeping in my car," I replied incredulously. "I'll freeze in there too! At least here I have a fireplace."

Greer quirked a stubborn brow.

"The fireplace is blocked, Della. No one has lived here since Nanna Delia, and it's been empty for over a year."

"This place is all I have," I told him, folding my arms across my chest when a strong gust of wind came in behind Greer. "I'm not sleeping in my damn car."

"Then you'd best make a plan," he replied. "Because you can't. Stay. Here."

I threw my arms up in defeat, already tired of arguing with this brute of a man. "I have nowhere else to go! I packed up my entire damn life to come here, okay? That what you want to hear? I'm here because my life fell apart in New York!" I didn't mean to say so much, or reveal why I came back, but something about the way he kept *barking* at me made me want to explode. It's not like I expected a red carpet welcome or anything, but *this*? He had no damn right. Asshole.

I rubbed at my temples, feeling the exhaustion of the day creep up on me from behind. When I opened my eyes, Greer was watching me, his gaze hot on my cool skin. His face was taut, skin stretched over sharp bone, and I could see the anger flashing in his eyes.

I sighed, suddenly very tired. "Just go, Greer. I can take care of myself." I'd been doing that for eleven years, and it wasn't about to change. I no longer had any family who could help me navigate this next part of my life. Only God knew where my mother was, but I'd been doing fine without her all my life.

Greer muttered something I didn't catch under his breath, but his hands were on his hips again. He passed me and stopped beneath the hole in my roof, peering up past the tree that had made the hole to begin with. He shook his head.

"We have a few places that need fixing. You see this…" He pointed at an exposed wooden beam. "…is one strong gust of air away from snapping into two and causing this…" He pointed to another, "…to give way and the tree to fully collapse into the house." He took a step forward, swiping his large hand from the tree to the ground. "If the tree falls, the bedrooms will have no access to this other side of the house, and you'll be trapped." He glanced back at me, a flash of worry crossing his face for only a second. "Until we can fix this, you can't stay here, Della. There's no way around it."

My frustration grew, forming a tight knot in my chest. What was I supposed to do now? The inn was at capacity with a wedding party, and our little town didn't have a hotel. And because I no longer had friends here, I couldn't shack up with someone else until my cabin was fixed. I was about to explain this to Greer, whether he listened was another story, but he spoke first.

"You'll have to stay with me if you have nowhere else to go."

My eyes widened. "That's not happening." What a ludicrous suggestion. He'd obviously lost his ever-loving mind.

"It's either my house or your car, and we've established you'll freeze in your car."

"I *really* can't stay here?" I asked incredulously.

Greer shook his head, his blonde hair falling over his forehead. "Nope." He popped the *p* and started for the open front door. His stride was confident, eating up the space in seconds.

Well, shit.

Of all the things I'd thought might happen when I finally arrived, this was not one of them. It was a terrible idea, but Greer had pointed out just how many options I *didn't* have. Leaving me with only one. Without saying anything else, he started wheeling my suitcases that were still by the door outside.

He packed his Jeep while I stood frozen to the floor. I brushed my fingers over my lips, my throat dry and my stomach twisting with discomfort. Greer came back for my last suitcase, and before he could walk out, I asked, "Are you even sure about this?" *This* being him having me stay with him.

He gave me a look, and I felt it *everywhere*. In the pitter-patter of my heart, the hollow of my belly. His green eyes full of so much of what he wasn't saying.

"I'm not thrilled you're back..." he admitted bluntly. The admission was like a sucker punch to the gut with a tire iron. "...but I'm not an asshole..." that was debatable at this point, "...and I'm not about to let you stay here and freeze to death either, Della. You can stay with me before Kyle and I get to fixing your cabin." He turned and walked out, and for a beat, I hesitated. Was I supposed to foll—

"You coming?" he hollered. "I don't have all afternoon to wait for you. We'll fetch your car later."

I blew out a harsh breath, resigning myself to this new turn of events. I grabbed my purse and followed him, not bothering to lock up. In a town like this, we never worried about locking our homes. It was pointless. Even more so because there was nothing of real value. And, well, I had a hole in my roof—locking up seemed redundant. By the time I slid into the passenger seat of Greer's Jeep, he'd already started the car and shifted it into drive.

Chapter 3

Greer

I shifted in my seat as I drove towards my cabin. I was only two roads up from her, where all the two-story cabins were located. It was the same cabin I'd grown up in, spent my whole life in, and now I'd told Della she could stay with me until Kyle and I managed to fix her cabin.

It wasn't the smartest thing I could have done, but Della was out of options. I was still reeling from the news of her arrival if I was honest with myself.

It'd been eleven years since she left, and I never thought she'd set foot in Kipsty again after she made it clear it wasn't enough for her. I recall the day she left like it was yesterday, and the old wound it had left behind was smarting because she was sitting beside me.

"Not much has changed," she remarked, looking out the passenger window before turning her big, blue eyes to me. Her gaze was hot on the side of my face, but I refused to look at her. I wanted to reply but came up short as to what to say.

I couldn't conjure up a single word in response, so I didn't even bother trying.

I turned up the steep road where my cabin was located at the very top. Della was right, though. Not much about the town had changed. The same could be said for the people, but Della would learn that soon enough.

I got to the top of the hill where my cabin sat on the border of the mountains surrounding Kipsty and stopped in the single parking bay on the side. It was semi-private, sitting on almost seven acres of land. The lights shone through the large windows, lighting the cabin from the inside. Without a word, I hopped out and started unpacking Della's suitcases. She came up beside me and took the smaller suitcases from the Jeep.

I carried them up the long staircase leading to the wrap-around porch, unlocked the heavy, solid wood front door, and dropped her bags in the foyer. She took tentative steps when she followed me inside, her gaze flitting around. I'd made many changes and idly wondered if she'd notice, or if she remembered what my home looked like when she'd spent so much time here as a teenager.

We were best friends once upon a time, and then we became more. Now though, we were practically strangers, and what? I was trying to be valiant by inviting her to stay with me? Idiot. It was a terrible idea, but it felt as though I suggested it on autopilot.

The words just came out of my mouth, unlike when I demanded what she was doing here. I knew exactly what I was saying *then*.

"You've made some upgrades," Della said quietly, and when I looked at her, it was like a haze had lifted. I noticed the changes, too. Dressed in dark denim jeans, beige riding boots, and a cream-colored puffer jacket, her blonde hair hung down her back in loose curls from beneath her beanie. She was always curvy, even when we were kids, but now, her hips flared, and her butt was fuller, muscular. I skirted past her ample chest, not wanting to gawk—I'd always had a particular obsession with her breasts.

I shook my head, berating myself for taking note of all things like they mattered. They didn't.

"Yeah," I sighed. "My ex-wife wanted to make it seem bigger," I replied, referring to how I'd raised the ceiling in the living room and added more windows overlooking the valley below that surrounded the cabins all the way down the road to Main Street.

Della's head whipped in my direction. "Ex-wife?" She exhaled. "You got married?"

I grunted in response. I didn't want to talk about Maisy and doubted Della wanted to either. I needed to get her settled in my guest room.

I trudged up the stairs and looked behind me to see if Della was following. I raised my brows at her when she wasn't, and it got her moving.

"You can stay in here," I told her, dropping her bags at the foot of the king size bed. "Sure you remember where everything is?"

She stood on the threshold and swallowed. "Your old room," she half-whispered. Her memory was good because we had four bedrooms upstairs, and this room had been mine. Though I wasn't sure how she'd remembered because none of my high school or college memorabilia adorned the walls anymore.

I couldn't help myself when I asked, "How'd you know?"

Her lips tilted in a half-smile, and she pointed to a spot beside the door. "Our initials." Huh. I'd forgotten about that. We'd carved out initials in the wood when Della was thirteen, and I was fourteen. It was before we started dating, too.

"Right." I cleared my throat. "Then I don't need to explain where everything is." I turned to leave, but Della stopped me, a delicate hand resting on my bicep. She blinked and looked up at me. In that moment, all I could focus on was the blue in her eyes that held so much of my past that it scared me.

"Thank you," she said softly. "For letting me stay here." I stared at her, gritting my teeth. "Can I, uh, make you some dinner?" she asked. I hadn't eaten, but I was planning to head into town to grab a bite to eat with Kyle. The thought of Della in my kitchen rankled me.

"I have plans with Kyle," I replied. I wasn't going to ask if she wanted to join us. "But help yourself to what you want in the refrigerator." I brushed past her, ignoring how her expression fell and walked back downstairs. I was ready to grab my keys and leave when I heard Della's phone ring from upstairs. Her voice was low and hard when she answered, and my curiosity got the better of me. I inched closer to the staircase and perked my ear.

"No, Alex, I'm not coming back," she hissed. The way her voice traveled, I could tell she was walking in a circle. Old habits die hard. It was a nervous tick.

"You *cheated* on me," she continued, her voice rising. "I'd skin myself alive before I even consider getting back together, so stop asking. Stop calling. I'm not coming back." There was a beat of silence and then a final, "We're *done,* Alex. There's nothing you can say or do to fix this, and honestly, I'm glad we're over. You wouldn't have made me happy, and if I made *you* happy, you wouldn't have cheated. So you can stop calling me."

I felt a little guilty for eavesdropping, and knew it was wrong, but I'd take any insight I could get as to why she'd come back. I just wasn't expecting it to be because her relationship had gone south. The irony wasn't lost on me, since Maisy had done the same thing.

Before I could hear anything else, I grabbed my keys and left, taking a quick drive down to Main Street and stopping curbside in front of *The Weary Traveler*—the lone bar-slash-restaurant in Kipsty. I spotted Kyle's pickup before walking in. It was busy, but that was nothing new. People either ate here or at the dinner down the road. I greeted a few people on my way to the bar, giving them a stiff smile. I'd known most of them my whole life, others I'd gotten to know when they moved here a few years back. People rarely ever left Kipsty, but over the last few years, we'd had to build more cabins to accommodate the people who decided they wanted to live here.

It was the Kipsty charm, as I called it.

We had tourists come in, fall in love with the place, and months later, they'd be here permanently.

He was sitting at the bar talking to Hayward, the owner. I sat down with a huff, removing my jacket and slipping it across the back of my chair.

"You're late," Kyle remarked, sipping his beer.

"Your usual?" Hayward the bartender asked. I nodded and turned to Kyle, his expression one of apprehension and expectation.

"So?" he asked without preamble.

I rolled my eyes. "I saw her," I told him. "Don't know why she's back, though."

"You were a dick, weren't you?" He surmised. He knew me better than anyone.

"I might have been," I admitted. "But she was stubborn as hell when I told her she couldn't stay in Nanna's cabin." I knew the cabin now belonged to Della, but the whole town knew that cabin as Nanna Delia's, and it would take a lot for that to change. "So, I told her she can stay with me until we get it fixed."

Kyle choked on a sip of beer, and I slapped his back. "You did what?" He wheezed. Hayward slid my Sam Adams in front of me and leaned on the counter with his forearms.

"We talking about Della Marie?" he asked.

Kyle pointed at me with his thumb. "Dumbass over here said she can stay with him until we fix Nanna's cabin."

Hayward hummed. "So, she's really back then?"

"In the flesh," Kyle replied, saving me from having to answer. "Anyone's guess as to why, though."

I didn't tell them about the conversation I'd overheard. Wasn't my place. Or my business.

"We'll have to fix her cabin sooner than scheduled," I told Kyle. "Can't have her in my house for too long."

"Not sure about that. We've got some emergency fixes scheduled over the next few weeks. And now that she isn't staying there and is safe at yours, fixing Nanna's cabin isn't quite an emergency, now is it?" Kyle said, smirking.

"You are loving this, aren't you?"

"Hey, I'm not the one who invited her to stay over. Why'd you do that again?" he asked.

"She can't stay in that cabin, and you know that," I reminded him. "It was either she freezes in the cabin, or she freezes in her car. Do you have any other suggestions other than her living with me?"

He was shaking his head when Daisy-May, the unofficial town matriarch, and diner manager, sidled up to us. She was dressed in a wildly colored kaftan; her firetruck red hair tied up in a beehive style straight from the 60s.

"Boys," she greeted in that airy voice, smiling wide at Hayward. "Greer, honey, how are you?"

I quirked a brow. I loved Daisy-May as much as anyone—she became Mamma Bear to all of us when Nanna Delia died—but the inflection in her tone gave her away.

"Fine," I replied, taking another sip of my beer. "Does *everyone* expect me to, like, fall apart or something?"

"We're just as shocked as you are that Della Marie is back," she replied warmly. "But we also know it'll hit a little differently for you." Ugh. I loved this town, but I hated how involved everyone was in each other's lives. It was a hazard of being such a small community, and nothing would change that. Everyone's life was up for public consumption, and tonight it was my turn, it seemed.

"It's no big deal," I lied. "Technically speaking, this is her home. Why she's back isn't anyone's business." I gave Daisy-May a look, and she *tsked*, waving me off.

"Leave it to me, honey. I'll find out why she's here." She winked and sashayed back to where all the old biddies were playing poker. Della had been in town for less than four hours, and I did not doubt in my mind that she was already the topic of *many* a conversation. And now I had no way of escaping her at all.

Chapter 4

Della

Snuggled in my navy-blue padded jacket, I slipped the faux fur hood over my head and walked down the road from Greer's cabin. I had been cooped up there for a few days and decided it was time to venture out.

The cabins were nestled in a valley, the trees covered in snow. My truck was safely packed in his driveway after he'd driven it over yesterday evening. I took a deep breath, reacquainting myself with the surroundings. It was still early, and if memory served me right, residents only surfaced around 9 a.m. I didn't sleep much the past few nights. I was in a somewhat strange place, and every sound woke me up.

Greer and I had been avoiding each other since he left me alone to figure out my way around his home. I had managed to entertain myself, and every morning, the fridge was freshly stocked with items I had used the previous day. Much as Greer was ignoring me, he wasn't going to let me starve. It was weird being in his cabin though, not only because of its sheer size but because, like Nanna's cabin, it held so many memories, good and bad.

As I walked, my breath came out in white puffs, and I tucked my mitten-covered hands in my pocket. I strolled until I hit Main Street and found myself in front of the diner. I looked at the sign and expelled a heavy breath.

Nanna had been gone over a year, and yet I could never bring myself to sell the diner either. Or change the name from *Delia's Diner* to something else. Though I wasn't here as the owner. I was here as a patron.

The bell chimed above my head when I walked in, and all heads turned to me. There weren't many people in yet, but hushed whispers filled the space all the same. I couldn't remember anyone inside, but they obviously remembered me. Daisy-May I remembered. She was running the diner in my stead and had taken over when Nanna died. Dressed in a bright yellow long-sleeve romper with ruffles around her neck and her red hair tied up in a side ponytail and yellow scrunchie, she glided over from behind the cash register. Her smile was wide, her arms outstretched.

"As I live and breathe," she said, her voice a light tinkle. Just as I remembered. She wrapped me in a warm hug and squeezed ever so tightly.

"You really are here, Della Marie." She pulled back and held me at arm's length, giving me a once-over.

"You're too skinny," she remarked, and I raised my brows. "But we can fix that."

She touched my cheek and led me to the empty booth, signaling a waitress to bring us some coffee. I sat down, and she followed, eagle-like eyes affixed to my face.

"How are you?" she asked. A young waitress stopped at our table and poured us both a cup of coffee before scuttling away.

I held the warm mug between my cold hands and blew over the top. "That's not what you *really* want to know, now is it, Daisy-May?" I smirked. "If I recall, you were never one to beat around the bush." Daisy-May was the kind of woman who called a spade a spade and had no problem speaking her mind. Nanna was much the same, and they were two women I'd always aspired to be like. I'd succeeded too, which is what made me so successful in my career. However, this was personal.

"Of course I want to know how you are," she replied airily. "It's been eleven years, Della Marie."

"Della," I corrected. "Just Della." I took a sip of my coffee and savored the hit of caffeine to my system. "You saw me at Nanna's funeral."

She huffed—a delicate sound compared to what I would have sounded like—and rolled her pretty blue eyes. "I hardly spoke to you that day, honey. You didn't want to know anyone that day." She wasn't wrong. Nanna's funeral was a haze. "Not that we blamed you, sweetheart," she added. "Losing Nanna Delia was hard on us all, but for you..." She trailed off with a shake of her head, making her 80s style ponytail swish from side-to-side.

"So..." I hedged, "...am I the talk of the town yet?" I glanced around and felt like I was an animal in a zoo exhibit.

Her gaze was soft but discerning. "You had to know you would be," she replied gently. "But everyone's curious as to why you'd come back after all this time?" It was a question I wasn't going to escape. I could evade it all I wanted, but at some point, it would come out, whether I liked it or not. Whether I wanted it to or not. It was also pointless trying to keep it a secret. Everything had a way of coming out in this town.

"I decided to take Nanna's cabin," I said, casting my gaze downward. "I needed a change of scenery, and when I decided to run away from my problems, this was the only place I could think of." I looked back up, and Daisy-May's expression was soft with compassion and understanding. She rested her hand on mine.

"You made the right decision, Della," she said, her tone as gentle as her countenance. "This was always home." I bristled but hoped she didn't see it. I hadn't thought of Kipsty Little Town as home in a long time.

As if remembering something, Daisy-May frowned and sat back the slightest bit. "Last I heard, Nanna's cabin was quite badly damaged after the last storm we had. Were Greer and Kyle finally able to fix it?"

I sucked my lips between my teeth and replied, "No." I sighed.

"I'm staying with Greer until they can fix it."

Her blue eyes widened, and her mouth made an O before she started forward and under her breath, murmured, "That Greer has grown up real nice, hasn't he?"

I walked into that one, and I knew it. But I wasn't going to lie about where I was living. They would find out soon enough anyway when people stopped by Nanna's cabin and wondered where I was.

I chuckled and tilted my head. "I suppose he has," I replied, laughing lightly. "He wasn't very happy to see me, though, so I was surprised when he offered to have me stay in his house until the cabin is fixed."

"Still has a good heart, even as a man," Daisy-May replied easily. "Can't imagine seeing you was easy for him." I hummed into my mug, taking a bigger sip of my coffee before replying, "That goes both ways, I guess."

"You know..." Daisy-May leaned forward, "...none of us were all that surprised that you left. You were always destined to do something big with your life." She cocked her head. "Did you? End up doing something big?" I gave it some thought.

"I suppose so, but I think it became too big, and too much. So, I quit, and left it all behind, kind of like I did with Kipsty when I was eighteen."

It was Daisy-May's turn to hum. "Funny how you ended up right back where you started, huh. All things come full circle eventually."

"The great, big circle of life," I remarked. "Have I missed much since I've been gone?"

Daisy-May laughed. "Not much has changed..." which I'd already guessed, "...the young ones have all grown up, and gotten married, and us oldies are just getting older."

I sucked my top lip into my mouth, latching onto the *married* part. Greer had an ex-wife. But I couldn't exactly press him for details.

"Greer mentioned he got married," I hedged, lifting my gaze to Daisy-May's. She wasn't smirking, not with her lips but with her eyes. "Said he has an *ex-wife?*"

"Right. He didn't tell you anything else?"

I shook my head. "He wasn't very talkative when he mentioned her," I shrug. "And I didn't want to pry."

"Well..." Daisy-May sighed, "...I may as well tell you since his *ex-wife* was a friend of yours and still lives in town with her *new* husband. Best you hear it from me, honey." She looked around as if to make sure no one else was listening, but we both knew they were. "Greer married Maisy Roberts, though she goes by Maisy Finch now."

I felt my eyes widen. My heart skipped a beat. Maisy was my best friend, and if I was honest, I always thought she liked Greer. It was always me, Greer, Kyle, and Maisy, though Maisy and Kyle never dated. But we were thick as thieves growing up. Maisy was the first person I called when Greer kissed me for the first time, asked me to be his girlfriend, and when I lost my virginity to him. And I had no right to feel any kind of way *now*, hearing that Greer had married her. But it still left a bitter taste in my mouth.

"Didn't last long," Daisy-May added. "Two years, maybe. And all they did was fight. She wanted babies a year after they got married, and he just wasn't interested. No one was surprised when they finally got divorced. Rumor has it he never really got over *you*, miss Della, and Maisy couldn't deal with it anymore."

"I hardly think that was it," I replied, finishing my coffee. "The Greer I knew would have married her because he loved her."

Daisy-May gave me a look. "Honey, that man changed the day you left, and he may tell you otherwise eventually, but he was just never the same. Seems you took his heart with you when you got on that bus and never looked back."

I huffed. "I highly doubt that Daisy-May. He must have gotten over me eventually."

She quirked a perfectly shaped brow. "Did you ever get over

him?"

I opened my mouth and then closed it. Had I gotten over Greer? I suppose feelings for Greer waned over time, but if I looked closely enough and examined how my heart broke when I left and how it stayed broken when I started my life in New York, I never did get over Greer. Not really. Daisy-May clucked her tongue as if she knew what I was thinking.

"You've probably fallen in love a hundred times over the years, Della, but our hearts..." she tapped her hand over her chest where her heart sat, "...they never get over that first time."

I hadn't fallen in love a hundred times since I left, but it was a nice idea. Preferable to the notion that I never got over Greer or that he never got over me. Did I love Alex? I wasn't even sure I could answer that. Things with him were still so convoluted. I couldn't bear to deal with that *and* being back in Kipsty Little Town.

Sensing my unease, Daisy-May switched topics and instead asked, "Have you had a chance to think about what you want to do with the diner?" No, the diner had fallen to the wayside, but before I could say that, Daisy-May sat forward again and added, "Because I have a business proposal."

The change of topic was what I needed to stop thinking about the whole Greer situation, and by the time I left, Daisy-May and I had agreed to be partners, though I was going to be the silent one. She'd buy fifty percent, and we agreed the name would stay. It wasn't what I intended to happen when I showed up this morning, but I was relieved to have it off my plate. Now I could focus on something else, like adjusting to small town living.

Rather than go back to Greer's house, I walked towards the cemetery and stopped in front of Nanna's headstone. The cemetery wasn't very big, so her spot was easy to find. I exhaled a heavy breath, wondering what Nanna would have said had I come home sooner before she had passed.

"Hi, Nanna," I started. "I guess you were right. I did eventually come back." I crossed my legs at my ankle, and tucked my hands in my jacket. "I'm not sure what I'm doing here yet, but I'm hoping the answer will come." My breath left my mouth in white puffs. "I miss you so much." My nose burned, but I didn't stem the tears that started. "And Greer wasn't too happy about me coming back, but I can't really blame him, huh?" I looked around, hoping no one could see me talking to a slap of stone like it held the answers to everything that had gone wrong in my life.

"Anyway, Kyle and Greer will fix up the cabin, but until then, I'm staying with Greer. Awkward, right? It was nice of him to offer, but I'm not sure he really wants me there. Hopefully, it won't be for long." I wiped my nose and tapped the top of the headstone. "I wish you were here." And I did. I needed her, even now, but I also knew she'd raised me to be strong and independent, and it's because of that that I knew I'd be okay here in Kipsty.

Chapter 5

Greer

The house was quiet when I walked in. I had no idea where Della had been all day, but Kyle and I had finally managed to assess the damage to Nanna's cabin a week after Della had arrived. The roof had collapsed into the living room courtesy of a large fir tree, which we needed to remove to see how much work the cabin needed before it was habitable again. It was going to be a bigger job than we'd anticipated, and I needed to talk to Della about the cost if I could find her.

What I did notice was that Della had cooked. She'd covered the food with a dishcloth and left a roast chicken in the oven at a low temperature to keep it warm, I assumed. I looked around, my stomach grumbling from the delicious smell wafting from the kitchen, but I couldn't see Della anywhere. I trudged up the stairs, and as I approached her room, I heard sniveling.

I raised my hand to knock but hesitated. I didn't want to see her tear-stained face. Even as a teenager, I couldn't handle seeing Della cry. I wondered if the game was true now, eleven years later, when we were both adults who had lives that were no longer entwined.

I heard another snivel.

Resting my hand on the door handle, I raised my hand again, and knocked.

"Della? You in there?"

There was a beat of silence, and then a muffled, "Yes. Dinner is downstairs if you're hungry." I wanted to be angry with her, keep pushing her away, but I wasn't going to let her stay in her room if she was crying.

"I'm going to open the door, okay?"

When she didn't respond, I pressed down on the door handle and slowly opened the door, poking my head in. Della was sitting on the floor at the foot of her bed, wearing a terrycloth robe with her wet hair piled atop her head and clothes strewn on the floor around her. She'd obviously been unpacking, and I surmised it wasn't the clothes or the unpacking that had her in such a state.

Splotchy skin, red, puffy eyes. It looked like she'd been biting her lip, too. It was swollen and irritated. She swallowed when her blue eyes landed on me, and I saw her chest heave with a deep inhale.

"You okay?" I asked. Whatever the circumstances around her return, I wasn't heartless. Something had upset her, and based on past experience, it took a lot to make Della cry.

"I'll be fine," she said, wiping her face with the sleeve of her robe. "You can go ahead and eat without me. I'm not hungry."

"You have to eat something." I sighed. "Besides, we need to talk about Nanna's cabin. Kyle and I assessed it today."

She blinked and looked around at her clothes. "I'm busy unpacking..." she trailed off and shook her head.

From where I was standing, it looked like she'd started unpacking but was interrupted. I had two choices. I could either leave her here and let her stay upset, or I could coax her into having something to eat and get her to calm down just a bit.

I stepped closer to where she was sitting on the floor and reached for her hand.

"C'mon, you need to eat, and we need to talk about Nanna's cabin."

She looked up at me again and placed her hand in mine so I could pull her up. The innate urge to pull her into my arms hummed under the surface of my skin, but I shook away the feeling and let go of her hand. She followed me out of her room and back downstairs to the kitchen. She took plates out, knives and forks, and I couldn't help but raise my brows when I saw she'd put together a fresh green salad and baked some bread rolls to go with the roast chicken in the oven. She took the chicken out, and I pushed her aside so I could carve it.

I cleared my throat. "Thanks for making dinner. You didn't have to."

"Figured you'd be hungry after working all day." She shrugged. "And it's the least I can do since you're letting me stay here." Her voice was flat, and the need to know what had her so deflated pulled at me. I was still curious as to why she was back, but I also couldn't bring myself to pry, no matter how badly I wanted to.

I set the table while Della dished up, and I didn't even wait for her to sit beside me before I started shoveling food into my mouth. I groaned appreciatively, trying to remember the last time I had a decent home-cooked meal.

"This is good," I mumbled around my food. I glanced over at her and noticed how she pecked at her own food. She caught me looking, and her expression turned sheepish.

"I can't eat when I'm upset."

Without thinking it through, I replied, "I remember." I finished my food and pushed my plate away, wiping my mouth with a napkin. "You want to talk about it?"

Della looked at me out of the corner of her eye, brows furrowed. "You really want to know?"

I lifted my shoulder. "If it'll make you feel better." I knew I'd done an about-face after showing up at her cabin a week ago like a raging bull, but I'd since realized I couldn't hold a grudge against her, no matter how hard I tried to.

It felt unnatural after so much time had passed. I'd stayed angry long enough after she left, and did my best to move on and let it go. And for the most part, I had. Obviously seeing her again conjured up some kind of feelings but staying angry was like waiting for rain during a drought. Useless and disappointing.

Della pushed her plate away, her food only half-eaten, and slumped in her chair. "My ex won't leave me alone," she started, fiddling with a napkin and tearing it into tiny pieces before laying them on the marble countertop in front of her. "I sold my event coordinating business, too, when I decided to come back." She shook her head. "Selling my business was the easy part, if I'm honest..." Her voice cracked, and she lifted her hand, wiping under her eyes. "Alex, my ex, cheated on me with his secretary." She turned her blue eyes to me. "Talk about a cliché, huh. And now she's p-pregnant." Her voice cracked, and seconds later, her face crumbled.

She covered her mouth to smother her sob, and my instincts took over when I wrapped an arm around her delicate shoulders and pulled her in for a hug. I even kissed the top of her head, and held her while her body shook.

Della was still kryptonite to me in so many ways, and I'd only come to that realization now that she was back. I hated seeing her upset. I wanted to comfort her, hold her, and promise her it would all work out—like I'd always done. Those same instincts came as naturally to me as breathing, and it didn't matter that I was angry with her for what she'd done years ago.

She pulled away and grabbed a new napkin to blow her nose before looking at me. "You said you assessed the cabin. What's the damage?"

I lifted my hand from her back and crossed my arms on the marble countertop. "There's a hole in the roof, as you saw, and the roof in the kitchen has a crack." I sighed. "We can fix it, but it will take some time. We have other urgent cabins that need to be fixed too. Some families are shucked up together, and we need to get to those in order of priority."

"How long will that take?" she asked, her voice scratchy from crying.

I blew out a breath and twisted so I was facing her. "Couple of weeks. We need to source some logs and a few other things, too."

Della sighed, her entire body slumping forward as she rubbed her hands down her face. "Couple of weeks," she muttered. "Shit. Okay, I can move into the inn. The wedding should be done by—"

"No!" I said abruptly, shocking the both of us. I cleared my voice before adding, "I mean, you can stay here until we're done. I'm okay with it...if you are," I told her. I didn't want her to worry about where she'd be staying while we fixed Nanna's cabin. I wasn't about to put her out on the street. "The cost is another thing we need to talk about."

Della nodded, looking straight at me. "And?"

I scratched the side of my face, worried about how she'd react when I told her. But she had to know. "A few thousand, at the very least. Our estimate from start to finish is about ten thousand dollars."

She didn't even blink when she replied, "That's fine. I made a whole lot more than that when I sold my business, and Daisy-May offered to buy half the diner a few days back." I felt my brows rise.

"You sold the diner?" It had belonged to Nanna Delia and was left to Della when Nanna passed. Daisy-May had been running it while Della was gone. The diner had been around since before Della and I were born, and it was a fixture in Kipsty.

"Half of it," Della replies. "We're partners, but she'll keep running it. I'm still trying to figure out what I'm going to do with myself."

I sucked my top lip into my mouth, contemplating how much I *could* ask without it seeming like I was digging for information.

"You said you sold your business," I hedged, waiting to see if she'd share some more with me. She wasn't obligated to, but I knew Della. At least I used to. Whenever she got upset, she needed a moment to gather herself, and her thoughts, before she spoke about it. She was a talker, and didn't like keeping things bottled up. I wondered if that had changed.

"And I thought you hated me," she countered, a half-smile edging up one side of her mouth. It seemed she was ignoring the direction the conversation was taking.

I huffed out a brusque laugh in spite of myself. "You know how I feel about surprises, Della." I hated them. It was a wound from my childhood, from when my parents were unexpectedly taken from me while I was 18. "And you are one hell of a surprise." Never in a million years did I think she'd come back. She was set on leaving, and she had stayed away for long that it was easy to assume she was never coming back.

"You might not believe me..." she started, "...but I came back because this was the only place I could come to. It was the first and *only* place I thought of when..." She looked down, swallowed, and shook her head. I gave her a minute to gather her thoughts.

"I couldn't cope anymore," she continued. She was opening up, and I could stop her and tell her I didn't care what her story was. But I did care and denying it was purposeless.

I was about to ask about the business she'd owned and sold to alleviate the tension between her shoulders when she said, "I was an event coordinator in New York. Had a very successful firm of my own after interning for a few years. And I don't know, my clients became more demanding, and I was working long hours even though I employed six people who worked for me. Then Alex, my ex, cheated on me with his secretary. We've been together for five years, but he started talking about marriage and kids and..." she shrugged a shoulder, "...it freaked me out. I couldn't picture my future with him."

She huffed out a breath and turned to face me, her eyes bright blue from shed tears. She wasn't crying anymore, though. "You asked me why I came back, and now you know."

I pulled my hands through my hair. "I'm sorry, Della. I really am. That's a lot for one person."

She let out a harsh burst of laughter. "I guess so. I keep asking myself if it's my punishment for leaving Kipsty in the first place," she said. "But then I think it's punishment for leaving you too."

Chapter 6

Della

I expected Greer to say something in response to my last statement, but he didn't. He regarded me, the look in his eyes indiscernible, and then looked away, clearing his throat.

"You should get some rest," he said. "I'll take you to the cabin when I can and show you what we intend to do." It was on the tip of my tongue to ask him about Maisy, but I bit back the urge and stood. I quickly packed the dishwasher and leftovers from dinner for Greer to take for lunch the following day. He disappeared upstairs at some point, presumable to take a shower and go to bed. I felt alone in his cavernous home, even though he was there.

Part of me regretted allowing myself to be vulnerable around him, but the other part, the larger part, felt safe enough to do it. If I could be vulnerable with anyone, it was Greer. Even after years apart, I still saw glimpses of the boy I'd left behind. Or maybe the young girl in me sought those parts out just to see if they still existed.

I went upstairs and back to the guest bedroom, sighing heavily when I saw the clothes on the floor that still needed to be packed away. I was staying here a few more weeks, so I might as well get comfortable and store away everything.

I shut the door, and leaned against it, counting my breaths until they evened out. Until I no longer felt frayed at the edges. I packed away my clothes, and zipped up my suitcases, placing them at the bottom of the wide cupboard that took up half the wall beside the bathroom door. After changing into my pajamas, I stared at the bed. I was exhausted but felt too listless to sleep. I hadn't brought a book to read, and my kindle wasn't charged. But I doubted I could concentrate enough to read anyway. My mind was jumbled after speaking to Alex an hour before Greer came home, after listening to him explain his indiscretion and indirectly trying to pin it on me. After speaking to Greer, and unintentionally spilling my guts, it all left me drained. I crawled into bed, and tried to sleep, tossing and turning.

At about 2 a.m., I heard a noise coming from downstairs, and after slipping my robe on, I opened my bedroom door. I padded my way down each step and rounded the corner to the sunken living room. A shirtless Greer was watching *Sports Center*, the Colts versus the Patriots. I leaned against the wall and watched him for a while, not saying anything.

His dream was always to play in the NFL, but he tore his ACL in high school. It wasn't long after that his parents died, and I remembered how much he'd changed after that. Sensing my presence, he turned his head, his gaze catching mine.

"Did I wake you?" he asked quietly. "I couldn't sleep."

I pushed off the wall and lowered myself onto the buttery leather sofa beside him. "Couldn't sleep either," I replied, tucking a strand of hair behind my ear. I pulled my robe around me tighter. "You mind if I just..." I hesitated, "...sit here for a bit?"

Greer's gaze was intense as his eyes tracked my features. But he shook his head and turned his attention back to the television. We watched silently, but I was content to just sit beside him.

Warmth radiated from his body, and I soaked it up. It was familiar but also new. Still comforting, though. But I didn't want to think too much about that. I looked around, thinking back to my conversation with Daisy-May, about Greer and Maisy, and tried, in vain, to find anything that would allude to a woman ever having lived here. There was nothing.

Greer caught me looking, and when I glanced in his direction, my cheeks warming from being caught, his brows were furrowed. "You looking for something?"

I bit the corner of my bottom lip and swallowed. "Signs that you were married," I replied softly.

Greer drew in a deep breath and let out on a sigh. "She took all her things when she moved out," he replied, looking at the television. I was waiting for more but that too was in vain because it became obvious he wasn't in a sharing mood. And I was far too curious for my own good. I contemplated just coming out with it, telling him I knew more, but then he'd know Daisy-May had spoken to me. And it felt like a gross invasion of his privacy.

"I can hear you thinking," he said dryly, making me snicker. He used to say just that when we were younger, when I had something on my mind but not the courage to say it out loud.

So, I went with it. "How'd you end up marrying Maisy?" I asked, waiting for some kind of reaction.

All I got was a droll look, and an almost imperceptible shake of his head. "People in this town talk too much," he muttered. He let out a breath. "'Spose you would have found out eventually," he continued. "Lasted almost two years, but we should never have gotten married." He cleared his throat. "I'd just graduated from college when we started dating, and I don't know, I guess proposing felt like the next right step. So, I proposed, and we got married." He shrugged. "Turns out she wanted more than I could give, and when the fighting became constant, she left." It sounded so simple when he put it like that. But knowing Greer, that's probably exactly how he remembered it. No frills or graces. It was so Greer.

"You must've loved her," I stated gently. "If you married her." I was in no position to judge or be jealous in any way. He had every right to move on, and I'd never begrudged him that. I was, however, shocked that it was with Maisy.

"I thought I did," Greer admitted. "But I was lonely after you left, and she was always there. Made a difference that we were at the same school and friend circle."

I nodded, a knot in my throat comprised of many emotions, but I didn't press for more information. I curled up on my side of the sofa and leaned my head on my hand. My eyes started drifting closed, and what I was sure was an hour or so later, I felt strong arms lift me and carry me up the stairs. I burrowed my face into Greer's bare chest, breathing in his clean, crisp scent. I felt weightless when he lowered me onto the bed and tucked me in. I thought I felt his lips brush my forehead, and I was sure I'd reached for him and asked him to stay. But it was all fuzzy in my state of sleepiness. I rolled over onto my side and snuggled into the warmth of the duvet.

***

Things between Greer and me became better. We would catch up over breakfast before he went to work or during dinner. Greer would tell me stories about the town and the people we went to school with—laughing at the happier moments and feeling a smidge of guilt at the sad times. It was great to hear what happened around Kiptsy Little Town when I was away. When I wasn't with Greer, I would explore the area or head over to the diner to speak with Daisy-May. I was slowly getting acquainted with my hometown, and more than once, I asked myself what would have happened if I hadn't left eleven years ago—a question I would pose to Nanna's grave when I visited to clean it up or replace the flowers with fresh ones.

Greer and Kyle were still pretty busy tending to the other cabins, but Greer would always take the time to pass by Nanna's cabin and let me know what else would be needed. Over the past two weeks, we had slowly built up a list of things that needed to be worked on when my cabin was next up.

I was looking out the window at the dreary, snowy weather one morning when I heard some movement from downstairs. I felt a warmth fill me, wanting to catch up with him before he left. It wasn't lost on me how I was beginning to enjoy this routine we'd found ourselves in. Then I heard voices, realizing he wasn't alone. The second voice, however, was female. My brows furrowed. I couldn't pinpoint who the voice belonged to, so I quickly changed into some warm clothes and made my way downstairs.

"I don't know what you're doing here, Maisy," Greer said harshly. I froze. Maisy was here?

"Wanted to see for myself that it was true," she replied haughtily.

Greer sighed. "See if what is true? Be specific. You know I hate word games." He was irritated, that much I could discern from the tone of his voice. I sucked in a breath and walked downstairs. Maisy's head whipped to the side when she saw me, her expression a mix of surprise and disdain.

She gave Greer an incredulous look. "So it's true she's *staying* with you?" She huffed.

"Hi, Maisy," I greeted, stepping towards Greer. I stood beside him, and without thinking about it too hard, I wrapped my hand around his bicep. I knew it was a possessive gesture, but it was obvious to me that Greer wanted Maisy to leave, and if I still knew Maisy in any way at all, it would make her mighty uncomfortable to see me show Greer affection. It always had.

She looked at me, her eyes ablaze with indignation. Though I didn't know why. She was married to someone else. She even had the obnoxious diamond on her left hand to prove it.

"Didn't take you long," she replied, lifting her nose in the air. She was shorter than me by a few inches and had to look up the slightest bit to meet my eyes. "Been here less than a month and you're already shacking up together?"

I quirked a brow.

"I hardly think it's any of your business where I'm staying."

Greer straightened beside me and folded his arms but didn't brush my hand away from his bicep. "You're wasting your time,"

Greer told her. "Della is staying here until we can get her cabin fixed, not that I owe you an explanation. You don't live here anymore."

Maisy made a noise in the back of her throat, her cheeks a ruddy red. Her eyes traced my features, and I knew that I was a threat to her at that moment. We were best friends once upon a time, so it wasn't a stretch to assume I still knew her tells. Her nostrils flared; cheeks puffed a little. Eyes widened.

"You have a lot of nerve showing up here," she told me. "We were all better off after Kipsty's Golden Girl left."

"You mean *you* were better off because you had a shot with Greer?" I replied coolly. I felt Greer's gaze on the side of my face, but I kept my eyes on Maisy. "Too bad you fucked it up."

She laughed derisively. "And now you think you can have him back? Is that it?"

"Not at all," I replied evenly. "Greer was just kind enough to offer me a place to stay for a while. I'll be out of here as soon as my cabin is done."

Before Maisy could offer up a pithy response, Greer continued, "Anything else I can do for you? Or are you just here to stick your nose where it doesn't belong?"

"I hardly think my return warrants a visit," I added, looking at Greer. He honed his gaze on Maisy.

I looked back at her. "You'll have to excuse us," I said lightly. "We have somewhere to be this morning, and I'm afraid we're going to be late."

I was lying, I had no idea what mine or Greer's plans were for the day, but Greer's disposition was clear to me. He didn't want Maisy here. And neither did I if I was being honest with myself. I knew I'd bump into her eventually, but not like this. And I certainly wasn't expecting to be met with such hostility when I'd done nothing to her.

"You should never have come back," she told me, her tone brazen with an undertone of bitterness.

I expelled a calm breath, using Greer as an anchor. "Well, I did, and I'm not going anywhere, so best you get used to seeing me around town with Greer." *With Greer* had its own implications, and the deliverance was done with intent. It implied she'd be seeing Greer and I *together*, which wasn't likely to happen, but, in that moment, it was exactly what I wanted her to think. If she wanted to show up unannounced with her claws on show, I could certainly unsheathe claws of my own.

Maisy opened her mouth and closed it again right before spinning on her heel, and walking out. As soon as she was gone, my shoulders sagged in relief, and I slipped my hand from Greer's arm.

"Good morning to you, too," I murmured under my breath. Greer shook his head, a small smile on his face.

"Glad to see you still have your backbone," he said quietly.

I glanced at him, and replied, "That was child's play compared to what I had to deal with in New York."

He hummed and stepped away.

"Your lunch is in the refrigerator," I reminded him. "There's enough for you and Kyle."

I tilted his chin. "Thanks. I was thinking of taking you to Nanna's cabin, and getting that list finalized so we can get to ordering."

"I'm ready to go when you are," I replied. "How about you take me to the cabin and we do one more run through? Then we can head to the diner and talk about it?"

Chapter 7

Della

I looked at the plans in front of me while Kyle—who'd decided to join us for a late breakfast—and Greer spoke about supplies and where to source them. Kyle, rather than Greer, had walked me through the cabin and showed me where the repairs were most needed. Hole in the living room aside, the roof in the kitchen had been weakened by the weight of the tree that had landed on the cabin and would likely need to be replaced.

A young waitress came over with our coffee and our food, so I slid the plans aside to make some space. Kyle dug into his food with gusto while my mind whirred about how long it would take before I could move out of Greer's place. I pushed my food around my plate, looking over the blueprints for my cabin.

"We'll have to remove the old roof completely," Kyle said, drawing my eyes up to him. "And then lay a new one. I found a place a few towns over that have the logs we use, and they can deliver as early as tomorrow."

I had a list in front of me detailing the cost of it all, including labor, and it was the one thing I wasn't worried about. I had enough money for the repairs and then some.

"It'll take about a week to get it sorted," Greer added around a mouthful of food.

I hummed. "How long would it take to remodel the whole cabin?" I'd seen some stunning ideas on Pinterest last week and decided that if I was going to live here, I might as well make some changes. "I mean, if you have the time for a remodel that is?"

Greer and Kyle exchanged a look before Greer said, "We've finished up with the emergency ones. Yours was the last one before we got back to our usual roster."

"We can definitely work on a remodel. I would love that. What did you have in mind?" Kyle asked.

I pulled my phone out of my pocket and opened the reference images I'd found. I slid the phone across to them, and their heads bent forward. Kyle whistled as they flipped through the images.

"I'll pay for it, obviously," I told them. "But if you're taking the roof off, we may as well do a redesign while you're at it."

"It'll take longer," Greer said, looking up at me. I interpreted his inference as *you'd have to stay with me for longer.* And maybe he didn't want that.

"I can move into the inn if it's too much," I told him. "I won't be in your hair for the duration of the remodel if that's what you're getting at." There was a frustrated bite to my tone. I wouldn't overstay my welcome when putting me up already seemed like an issue. He frowned.

"That's not what I meant, Della."

I was about to reply when Daisy-May floated over to our booth, coffee pot in hand. She was dressed in a fuchsia pink tracksuit, and white and gold Nike high-top sneakers. Her red hair was braided over her shoulder.

She poured us more coffee without us having to ask, and when she didn't walk away immediately, I looked up at her.

"Della, sweetheart, you're in the event planning business, aren't you?" I *was,* but I didn't tell her that. Besides, she didn't give me the opportunity to say so before she spoke again. "We have our annual Christmas Market as you know, beginning of next month, and Maisy usually plans it, but she opted out this morning looking rather..." Daisy-May licked her lips and looked down at me, "...*annoyed,* and said she wouldn't be able to plan it this year. I was wondering if you'd be able to help."

I remembered the annual Christmas market. People in town set up stalls in the town square and sold a variety of things. It brought a lot of tourism to Kipsty, and outside of Christmas and New Year, it was one of the biggest events of the year. Nanna had a stall every year and sold sherpa blankets, homemade quilts with a fleece interior, knitted beanies, and mittens. I sucked my lips between my teeth, mulling it over. I didn't have anything better to do with my time right now, and it was hardly the same as planning a high society event like a gala or a celebrity wedding.

"Sure," I replied, giving her a wide smile.

"Wonderful." She smiled appreciatively. "It's a bit last minute, with less than three weeks to go. We should get started as soon as possible, so while the boys do whatever they're doing, I'll bring over the list of this year's participants, and you can come up with the rest."

I opened my mouth, but she was gliding away before I could say anything.

Kyle chuckled. "You've gone and hopped yourself into something now, Della Marie." He shook his head, a smile on his face. "But I have a feeling you'll do a better job than Maisy did. Last year's was a near disaster, and if we can make it better this year, maybe we can get some newcomers visiting the town."

Greer cleared his throat but didn't tell Kyle that Maisy had paid us a visit earlier, and that was probably why she'd been so *annoyed* when she came to the diner. I sat back.

"So…" I hedged, "…can you make the changes I want to the cabin?" I was hoping they could. It was dated, and I wanted to make it my own as much as I loved it for several reasons. And I knew Nanna would want the same.

Kyle scratched his head and took the pencil from behind his ear. He made some notes on the blueprints before explaining, "I'll have to draw up new plans, but I'm pretty sure we can do it."

"Great," I sighed. "I'll go pack up and move to the inn until you're done redoing the cabin."

I noticed Greer's glower but didn't comment on it. Kyle finished his breakfast and slid out of the booth. He knew breakfast was my treat. "I'll get a start on this..." he said, looking between Greer and me, "...and get back to you as soon as I have new plans. See you later?" he asked Greer.

Greer nodded, and we watched Kyle leave just as Daisy-May walked over, a file thick with papers in her hands. She dumped them in front of me with an audible exhale. "Applications have already been approved for each stall," she explained. "But that's as far as Maisy got. We don't have a theme, or decor ideas, or anything else."

"I'll figure it out," I assured her. "Do you have the layout of the town square in here, too?"

"It's all there," she replied. "You're a lifesaver, Della." She winked, and I called for the check a few minutes later. I left some cash and a tip and then left the diner with Greer.

He was quiet as we walked towards his Jeep, and then he stopped so abruptly I walked into him with an *oof*.

He spun to face me on the sidewalk outside the diner. "Why do you want to remodel the cabin?"

My brows furrowed. "Because I need it updated," I replied simply.

"So you can leave again?" He sounded angry, and his conclusion flummoxed me.

"Wha—" I shook my head and blinked. "How'd you come to that conclusion, Greer?"

"It would make sense," he replied harshly. It was a sharp juxtaposition to his mood earlier that morning. "Fix it up, sell it for a profit, and then leave."

I exhaled through my nose and pursed my lips. "I'd like to remodel it because, like I said, it's dated and in need of a facelift. But not so I can sell it. I'd like to *live* in it." When he didn't respond immediately, I added, "I'm not leaving, Greer." He glared, and I glared back. I knew he didn't believe me, but did I need him to? The scary answer was that I wasn't sure. "I don't owe you an explanation—"

"Yes," he snapped. "You do. You waltz back into town like nothing ever happened like you didn't leave, and now you're pretending like it never happened." Suddenly, I knew where this little fit was coming from. I thought we'd made the slightest bit of headway this past few weeks, but clearly, I was wrong.

I stepped into his space, looked up into his blazing eyes, and in a low voice, said, "I remember *everything*, Greer. And I regretted it for months, *for months,* before I made peace with my decision because I knew I'd done what was right for *me*." I looked around, aware that we weren't alone, before looking back at Greer. "You're angry, and to some extent, I understand it, but it was *eleven years* ago, and I've let it go. Have *you*?"

His nostrils flared, and he scowled, but rather than answer me, he tossed his house keys at me and muttered, "Don't wait up for me." I watched him climb into his Jeep and drive away in the direction of my cabin. He was most likely meeting Kyle there later, but either way, he was angry, and it was because of me.

Before heading back to his cabin, I passed by the Inn, only for my plan to be tossed out of the window. There would be a corporate retreat in two days and they'd booked out the entire place for two weeks, and after that, another wedding party. I didn't ask if there'd be room after, already reading the receptionist's face. With Christmas coming up, they were probably booked up until the new year.

Just my luck. I have nowhere to go.

It was a bit of a walk to Greer's cabin, and by the time I got to his cabin, I was panting. I wasn't out of shape by any stretch of the imagination, but it was the altitude.

I unlocked the front door and went straight to the spacious dining area, dumping the file Daisy-May had given me on the rectangular dining room table. Greer could spend the day sulking if he wanted to, but I wasn't going to linger on the past and beat myself up over it all over again.

I'd done that already.

However, if Greer wanted more of an explanation as to why I left all those years ago, then he needed to man up and come right out and say it. I wasn't going to grovel, and considering I was stuck here for the next month or two, there was no point in wallowing in guilt for that long. I took a moment to calm myself down since I'd spent the walk up here mulling over Greer's frustration with me and not having alternative accommodation.

After a quick flip-through of the file, I realized I was going to need a few things from my former office. I sent a text to my ex-assistant and asked her to send what I needed to my new address, then I started searching online at stores in the nearby town that would have what I was looking for. Last year's theme was Winter Wonderland, and all I could do was roll my eyes. Maisy wasn't the most original. Never mind. I'd make sure this year's market was the best the town ever had. And I'd deal with Greer later.

I started by searching on Pinterest, much like I had for cabin remodel ideas, and made notes. I lost myself in my task, like I had with prior events, but rather than be filled with anxiety or dread over a particular event, I was excited about it. Excited to do something that was a tradition in Kipsty. Once I'd settled on a theme, I made a list of what I would need and started looking at where I could find it. It'd mean a drive into Denver, and maybe that's what I needed. It would put a little distance between Greer and me, and I wasn't sure that was a bad thing.

Chapter 8

Greer

"You're grumpier than usual," Kyle remarked as we unloaded the lumber we'd gotten in Boulder for Della's cabin. Kyle had amended the plans, and three days later, we were ready to start remodeling.

After Kyle showed me the pictures he'd received from Della after breakfast, I could admit Della had an eye for design, and what she had in mind for her cabin was quite stunning. Not that I could admit that to her after my outburst. Pretty sure she wasn't going to be speaking to me after that. But hell, I sat in that diner, my mind reeling with memory after memory of us being there together, and suddenly, I had this unsolicited anger boiling behind my sternum.

I wanted to know right then and there why she left. And not why she left *Kipsty Little Town*, but why she left *me*. I thought I'd made my own peace with it, had lived with the knowledge that I may never know the truth for years, but the simplicity of just being near Della again brought it all back. And now I had to know. Admittedly, she didn't deserve my outburst, but the anger in my veins was because of her, and directing it *at* her felt justified. To me, at least.

"She getting to you?" he asked when I didn't reply. I looked up at him, hands on my hips. "I mean..." he continued, "...I was shocked when you told me she's staying with you and wondered how long it would take before you snapped. Have you snapped?"

I adjusted the gloves on my hands and lifted a log onto my shoulder. "I might have lost it after breakfast the other day," I admitted begrudgingly. "After you left. Been giving her the cold shoulder for the past three days." I carefully climbed the ladder and slid the log between two others that were still part of the original roof structure. Because it was flat, we'd replace one log at a time, starting with the roof. I twisted at the hips and gestured for Kyle to hand me the next one. We'd already removed the damaged logs, and if we worked efficiently, the entire roof would be done by the time we called it a day.

"Don't blame you," Kyle said after handing me the last log. He leaned against the ladder. "Has to be hard having her in your house, too."

I was still getting used to it. I lived with Maisy for three years, two of which we were married, but having her in my space never left me restless or uneasy. Like my skin was shifting over my muscles, over bone. Nearly a month of feeling this way had left my system out of whack.

"She's pretending like nothing happened," I told him, if only out of irritation. "Breezes into town and expects everything to just be *normal* like she didn't leave me at all."

Kyle let out a puff of air. "Why don't you just talk to her?"

Good question. Why *hadn't* I just asked her, in a civilized manner as opposed to snapping at her, why she left *me*? I knew why she left Kipsty, even if I didn't understand it, but she never said why it was *me* she chose to leave. Kipsty wasn't enough for her back then, but did that mean I wasn't enough either? The more I thought about it, the angrier I got.

I climbed the rest of the way up the ladder and positioned the logs before grabbing the drill. I took my anger out on the wood, pressing the drill harder than necessary, but it was better than talking about my goddamn *feelings*. Kyle climbed up behind me and checked my work, making sure nothing was loose.

"Looks good," he remarked. "I have a new blueprint for her remodel, and I actually like what she's going for." I only caught a glimpse of the pictures before we drove here, but if Kyle said it looked good, I believed him.

It was well past five when we were done. I helped Kyle load his pickup and then headed home. The lights were on when I arrived, and when I walked in, it was quiet. Della had chosen to set up camp in the dining room, papers and files strewn about with a whiteboard full of her scribblings in front of it. I had found her here the past few days, but she was nowhere to be found today.

As I approached the staircase, I heard her singing, and it was coming from her room. It took me back to when she used to sing in the shower and also reminded me of the showers we often took together without Nanna knowing. Though I was sure she knew, just like she knew we were having sex. There was always a box of condoms in Della's bedside drawer, and I knew she didn't buy them.

I was dragged from the recollection by a shrill scream, and without thought, I stormed into Della's room and blew into her bathroom. She was staring in the corner of the large shower, on the opposite side of the shower head.

She turned as soon as she saw me. "S-spider," she sputtered, pointing to the corner of the floor. I froze for a moment, taking in her womanly shape. She didn't think to cover her front in her state, and I was blessed with a good look at the woman she'd become. Perky, fleshy breasts, her pink nipples erect from the slight chill to the air. She had a soft belly with a slight curve at her waist. A look at her well-trimmed pussy drove blood straight to my core. My cock twitching drew me out of staring at her.

I couldn't remove it or even look at it if Della was naked, so I grabbed a towel, wrapped it around her, and picked her up. I moved her out of the shower and then shut the water off. In the corner was what looked a whole lot like a Wolf spider. They were common in these parts and harmless but scary looking because they resembled a Tarantula. I coaxed it into my hand and let it out the bathroom window.

Della was still shaking when I faced her, and I remembered she had arachnophobia, and for her, the fear was debilitating. She shook, eyes wide.

"You okay?" I asked gently. Without thinking about it too hard, I approached her and started rubbing my hands up and down her arms.

"S-sorry," she murmured, looking up at me, her wet hair still sudsy from her shampoo. "C-can you m-make sure there isn't a-another o-one, p-please?" Her lips trembled, and her eyes grew wet. I licked my lips and forced myself to keep my gaze trained on Della's face and not look lower. I checked to make sure there were no more spiders and closed the window in case another one wandered in from the cold outside.

"You're safe," I told her. "All gone."

She nodded but didn't make a move to step back into the shower. "You should finish up," I told her, gentling my tone despite how rankled I was earlier. I caught sight of her long, tan legs and swallowed when images of what I had seen higher flashed in my mind.

"Can you leave?" She squeaked out. I stared at her a beat and then nodded. I tried the door handle, but to no avail. I yanked and pulled, but the door had closed while I was taking care of the spider and now it was stuck.

"Fuck," I muttered under my breath, trying again.

I rested my forehead against the door as Della quietly asked, "What's wrong?"

I almost didn't want to tell her. Not only did she have arachnophobia, but she was also horribly claustrophobic.

"Door's stuck," I mumbled, looking at her from over my shoulder.

"Try again," she said, her eyes darting between my face and the door handle. I tried again, but it still wouldn't budge.

"You have to be kidding," she said, her voice turning shrill. "This can't be happening, Greer." Her panic rose. "Get it open."

"Della, I need you to breathe. I can get it fixed, okay?" My third and fourth attempts proved just as fruitless as my first and second, and I knew Della was watching.

"Are we stuck?" she asked, panicked more now than she was ten minutes ago. "Greer, we can't, we can't—" Her breathing grew labored, and past experience told me she was having a panic attack. She shook her head vigorously, her breathing choppy, and her eyes widened. So, I did what I thought would calm her down the fastest and closed the gap between us before pressing my lips to hers.

My hand cupped the back of her head, and I held my breath, hoping the kiss would distract her. I'd used it in the past, and it worked because it made Della hold her breath which stopped the panic attack. However, it backfired because the feel of her mouth on mine distracted *me*. She relaxed into me, and though her breathing evened out, we didn't pull apart. I didn't stop kissing her, and she didn't stop kissing me.

Chapter 9

Della

I hated two things more than anything else in this world. Besides my ex. Spiders and being trapped in a small space. But I was less focused on those two things and more focused on the feel of Greer's mouth on mine. His lips were soft and pliable, and I liked the feel. It distracted me from everything else.

I expected him to pull away when my panic receded, but he didn't. I could have, but now that he had his mouth on mine, I didn't want him to pull back. I flicked my tongue to the seam of his mouth and felt his lips part. Tentatively, I slid my tongue into his mouth, and every nerve ending and cell in my body came alive when his tongue slid against mine. I sighed into his mouth and stepped towards him, feeling the length of his tall, hard body against mine.

I clutched my towel against me with one hand and used the other to grip the nape of Greer's neck. My fingers tussled his hair. He moaned into my mouth, and it lit my body up from the inside. He slanted his head, changing the angle of our kiss, and licked the inside of my mouth with fervor. Something about it felt angry, but I soaked it up anyway, injecting my own anger into how I pulled at his hair.

Our teeth clashed, but that didn't deter us. I startled when his hand landed on my hip and moved around my back, his palm flat as he pushed me closer. It was like a trip back in time, kissing

Greer, except his once boyish hands were replaced by those of a man, and his once unsure movements were replaced by confidence and willfulness. He was taking and giving and I was giving and taking, a familiar, but also new, exchange.

In an uncharacteristic display of courage, I dropped the towel between us, hearing it *thud* on the floor. Greer pushed me until my back hit the wall, and then lifted me, my legs going around his waist.

"Jesus," he muttered into my mouth. "Della." I was breathless, but this time it wasn't because of a panic attack. I whimpered when I felt the seam of Greer's denim between my legs, and the hardness behind his zipper. It was tantalizing, all the sensations happening all at once and my heart hammered away in my chest like it was staging a jailbreak.

Greer's phone started ringing, and we both froze, his forehead on mine.

"Fuck," he muttered, rolling his forehead on mine. Keeping me pinned to the wall, he reached into his pocket and frowned. "It's Kyle," he said, his voice hoarse. "If the door's stuck, I'm going to need his help." His eyes met mine, and I hoped the moment was on pause and not over. Slowly, Greer lowered me to the ground but kept his arm around my bare back.

So much for being upset with him.

"Kyle, hey," he answered, his dark eyes on me. I could hear Kyle's voice on the other end, but what he was saying was indiscernible. "Yeah, can you come to the house? Della and I are, uh, locked in the bathroom attached to my old bedroom. Door is jammed shut." Kyle said something, and Greer shook his head, a small smile playing at his lips. "Shut up, asshole, and just get here, okay?" He hung up and bent to grab the towel. He wrapped it around me, his eyes taking in my naked body. I didn't mind, and I wasn't shy. Greer had seen me naked more times than anyone else, even if we were teenagers. He looked at the door, and then at me.

"About the other day…" he started, "…I shouldn't have lost it like that with you." If he was trying to distract me, this was a pretty effective way to do it. God only knew how long Kyle would take to get here, so we may as well talk. I licked my lips and almost dropped my towel when I touched my mouth with my fingers. They were puffy and a little swollen, which spoke to the heat of our kiss. My brows knitted.

"I never meant for you to feel like I left you, but I understand why you did," I said, a slight tremor to my voice. I was starting to get cold and still needed to finish my shower. And that wasn't happening while Greer was trapped in the bathroom with me.

"I thought I wasn't enough," he started, still looking down at me. He touched my cheek, and I shivered, my skin breaking out in goosebumps. "I thought it was me, Della." I was shaking my head before he finished his sentence.

"It had less to do with you, and more to do with what I wanted and couldn't find here. But I knew leaving Kipsty meant leaving you, and trust me, it wasn't an easy decision." I'd cried myself to sleep many a night because even though I was chasing a bigger life than Kipsty could offer, I missed Greer fiercely. He wiped my cheek, and I realized I'd started crying. For him. For me. For us. For the time we lost.

"I regret leaving *you*," I whispered. "Every day. But leaving Kipsty was what I needed, Greer." I let out a breath. "Kipsty was too small, and I felt trapped here, but when I was with *you*, I always felt like I could fly. And then you left for college, and I was stuck here. You came home on weekends, and I knew college was important to you, but you were gone more than you were here, and most days, I felt like I was losing my mind being here alone. Can you see that? After all this time, can you try and understand?"

He opened his mouth but was cut off by a sharp knock on the door. That was fast. Then again, because Kipsty was so small, Kyle could be here in less than ten minutes, regardless of where he was coming from. For all I knew, Kyle was on his way over anyway.

"You guys okay in there? All decent?" His voice was more amused than concerned. "I'm going to jimmy the lock with a screwdriver, see if that works, okay?"

Greer looked at the door. "Okay," he replied gruffly. He positioned himself in front of me, and after a bit of noise, and effort on Kyle's part, the lock clicked, and the door sprung open. He stuck his head in.

"All fixed." He grinned when I peered around Greer. "You'll need to replace the lock," he explained, holding it in his hands. "Until then, you won't be able to close the door."

"Thanks, man," Greer replied, keeping me behind him. When Kyle didn't make a move to leave, Greer cleared his throat. "You mind?"

"Sure." Kyle chuckled. When he was gone, Greer turned. "Finish up in here. I'll leave the bathroom door open, but close your bedroom door, okay?"

I nodded, and he placed a kiss on my forehead before walking out. I heard the shut of my bedroom door and sagged against the wall. I played our kiss over and over again in my head, even while I showered and changed into my pajamas. When I made my way downstairs, Kyle was gone, and Greer was leaning against the window in the living room.

"Hey."

His head snapped in my direction. "Hey. Feeling better? Kyle dropped off some dinner too. It was his but he insisted we had it." Because I had the kiss playing in my head on a loop, I wasn't hungry. Not for food anyway. My body was still vibrating with unspent desire, and it all started with a kiss. Well, not just any kiss. It was because Greer kissed me. And it held both promise and precious memories from our youth.

I knew Greer as a young man, someone who, like me, was finding his way. But I wanted to know him as a man, as who he was *now*. And I found myself wanting him to know this version of me.

"I'm not hungry...for food," I said, something within me snapping. My entire body was still vibrating.

The tension between us tightened for a second before he pushed off the windowsill and approached until he stopped in front of me. I looked up and felt my pulse skitter beneath my skin.

"I'm sorry," I murmured. "For ever making you feel like you weren't enough. Because you were, you always have been, Greer." He took in a sharp breath, and then his mouth was on mine. We were rushed and uncoordinated. Greer picked me up. I threw my pajama top off en-route to his bedroom and unbuttoned his shirt, leaving it on the floor.

He walked into his bedroom, and the entire space smelled like him. I didn't even bother looking around. My mouth fused to Greer's. He laid me on the bed and, without any finesse at all, removed my pajama pants and white lace panties.

Should have come down in a towel? Would have been faster.

I pressed my knees together while Greer removed his denims and boxer briefs and watched as he spread my legs. He leaned over me to the bedside table and grabbed a condom, tearing it open with his teeth. And *then* I looked. His cock was hard and thick, a vein running on the underside that stood out as it wound its way to the head.

Greer slid the condom on with ease and flicked his gaze to me while rubbing hot hands against the outside of my thighs. I squeezed a breast in my hand, primed for him. There was no time for foreplay. We needed this—now!

Inhaling a stuttered breath, my eyes traced his chest, his perfectly shaped pecs, his staggered abdominal muscles, and the pronounced V that led to his shaft. I licked my lips and squeezed my insides. I let out a squeak when Greer pulled me closer and roughly flung my legs to the side. He took his cock in his hand, sliding his hand up and down before pressing the head through the lips of my sex, over my swollen clit. I shivered when I felt him press himself to my entrance and knew, from the gleam in his eye, that this was going to be hard and fast, and that's what he needed, what I needed too.

Lifting my hips, he slid in just an inch, and slid out before snapping his hips forward. My back bowed off the bed as he filled me, and I let out a soundless mewl, my mouth hanging open as I adjusted to his size. He muttered curses under his breath, using a finger to rub my clit. I sighed out a heavy breath as my body lowered to the bed, and when I looked up, he was looking down at where he filled me. I lifted my hips, and he slid out the slightest bit but slid back in when I moved my hips down again. He crouched over me, stealing a kiss before he started thrusting. I grabbed the bedding until my knuckles were white and inhaled our sounds while Greer set a punishing pace.

"Oooh," I moaned into his mouth, grabbing hold of his neck with one hand. "Please," I begged, already close to that glorious precipice. Greer grabbed my butt cheeks and held me still as he snapped his hips faster and harder. My toes curled, and I cried out when he sucked a pebbled nipple into his mouth.

"Yes, yes, y-yes," I chanted, and then gritted out a, "Fuck." He wasn't slowing down, and I was fast approaching the cliff, anticipating the fall.

"Come with me," I breathed. His gaze flicked up, and he moved from my nipple to my mouth.

"Mine," he murmured before sliding his tongue into my mouth. He thrust his hips and stayed still as we crashed over the edge into an oblivion of stars and explosions. My body felt warm all over as I shook, arching my back and letting my legs fall to the side. Greer gripped my throat and grunted into my mouth. He panted, his body vibrating with his release, inadvertently giving me a second orgasm.

My heart felt too big for my body, my lungs working overtime for air. I slid my hands into Greer's hair and pulled, closing the small space between us until I could feel his heartbeat against my chest.

That was an angry fuck. No two ways about it.

The thought, however, made me smile against his lips.

"Feel better?" I teased, breathless. He grinned, knowing I'd caught him out, and nodded.

"I don't remember it being like that," he replied, gaze probing.

A burst of laughter came from deep in my chest, and I replied, "We know what we're doing this time." And it was the truth. We fumbled *a lot* when we experimented as teenagers.

"The question is..." I added quietly, a challenge in my tone, "...whether your stamina is the same." Greer was insatiable when we were dating, and so was I. But there was something to be said for time and experience, and the opportunity to mature.

Greer kissed the side of my neck and sucked, leaving a mark. He'd always done it, and I was secretly thrilled he still did. "Let's find out," he replied, reaching for the bedside table and rolling us so that I straddled him.

Game on.

Chapter 10

Greer

Della had her bare leg thrown over mine, her head on my chest as I trailed my hand down her spine, counting the bumps in my head. My floor-to-ceiling windows gave us a spectacular view of the snow falling steadily outside and the big, fat moon in the sky. She sighed, her warm breath fanning over my chest. I turned my head and kissed her forehead, enjoying the feel of her tucked against me and in my arm. She slanted her head to look up at me and gave me the sweetest smile before looking back out the window.

"Tell me about New York," I murmured. "About your business." It seemed a safe topic now that we'd used each other's bodies to get out the pent-up frustration and dormant anger and regret.

"The city is beautiful," she replied softly, nuzzling closer. Any closer and she'd end up under my skin. Not that I'd mind. It felt as though she'd been living there for years, even when were apart. It was the reason Maisy and I never worked out. Because she wanted a place that belonged to Della, and I was a fool to think it could ever belong to anyone else. "It's a hive of activity, and it's true that it's the city that never sleeps. The energy is addictive and loud, and I loved it."

I heard her take a breath before inhaling my own, savoring the scent of her and me mixed together. Sweat and sex and something sweet. "I loved the pace of it all and feeling small compared to everything around me." I tried to picture her there, and the truth was, I could because I'd seen her.

"I saw you once," I admitted in the quiet of my bedroom. I felt her gaze on me but didn't meet her eyes. "I wanted to see you," I sighed. "See for myself that you were happy, and the day I saw you, you were walking down Fifth Avenue with a friend, I think, and you were laughing and smiling, and then I knew I had to let you go. It was about a year after you'd left." I begged Nanna Delia for weeks to tell me where Della lived, where she worked, anything. And at first, she wouldn't tell me. Eventually, she caved in. "Nanna Delia told me that you liked to go get a mid-morning coffee at Bluestone Lane's Upper East Side Café every day of the week before going back to work. I caught the first flight after that."

"Why'd you never say hello?" she asked. Her tone wasn't accusatory. Just curious, if not a little surprised.

I sighed. "Because I could see you were happy, Della. You were with a few people and seemed to be in your element. And I wasn't going to ruin it by showing up out of the blue." I relaxed when I felt her head drop back to my chest. "As long as you were happy, I could cope, you know?"

"I was happy," she admitted. "The people you saw me with were other interns I worked with. It was my first job at an event coordinating firm, and as hard work as it was, I fell in love with my work." She rubbed my chest, and my skin broke out in goosebumps. But I loved the feel of her hand on my skin.

"Three years later, I decided to go out on my own and start my own firm. I took those same friends with me, and one of them became my assistant." I felt rather than saw her smile. "We planned some of the most extravagant events, Greer. Galas and fundraisers for the city's elite, and that's how I built my business. I networked with all the right people, who referred me to more people, and soon I was planning birthday parties for the children of famous athletes and celebrities." She shifted and rested her chin on my chest, her arm around my ribs.

The moon caught her eyes, and they looked icy blue in the light. Her blonde hair was a mess, but she looked beautiful. Ethereal, really. Otherworldly. And I was a mere mortal, soaking up her essence. Her brows knitted then, and I lifted a hand to smooth the frown away with my thumb.

"I'm not sure when I stopped loving it," she said. "It started taking more and more out of me, and at some point, it stopped feeding my soul. I started feeling restless and unsettled. Ungrounded, I guess. And when Nanna died..." she exhaled, "...I asked myself if it was what I still wanted. If being in New York was still what I wanted." I felt the lift of her delicate shoulder. "I got engaged shortly after Nanna died, but that also felt wrong. I thought it was because it was just such a big step to commit to someone for the rest of my life when it was someone else I'd always envisioned my future with."

My heart stuttered in my ribcage.

"I could never admit Alex wasn't the one..." she continued, "...but it felt like it was the *right time*, the *next step*, so I went with it, thinking those feelings would pass." She sucked her lips. "Then he cheated, and as much as that hurt me, I wasn't nearly as upset as I should have been. So, I took it as a sign, and decided I was done with all that. I sold my business and apartment and packed it all up to return to Kipsty."

She tilted her head, laying her cheek on my pec.

"It was the first decision in a really long time that felt right. I *knew* it was what I needed, but I also knew it wouldn't be temporary." She huffed out a laugh. "The last time I saw Nanna before she died, I was so unhappy, and no longer had a clue what I was doing, and she said to me it would be over soon enough because Kipsty was calling." She shook her head. "I only figured out what she meant when I ended up in a damn ditch ten minutes from town."

Her hand rested on my stomach, and Della started playing with my fingers when I said, "You're the reason Maisy and I never worked out."

She frowned, and this time I didn't wipe it away. "What do you mean?"

I shrugged. "She wanted to fill a space that was yours, and when she started talking about having a family, I switched off. I'd only ever imagined having a family with one person my whole life, and that was you. She tried to trap me a few times, did some crazy things, but when she never fell pregnant, we started fighting more until I couldn't take it anymore. I filed for divorce and ended it."

Della swallowed, the shadow of her throat moving. "I'm sorry, Greer. That must have been hard on you."

"Not any harder than being cheated on," I replied. She leaned forward and pressed her lips to mine. It wasn't seductive, or a segue to something more. She was kissing me to make it better. I cupped the back of her head, and held the kiss a little longer, just because I could.

I relaxed back into the mattress, and then asked, "Did you make any decisions about the Christmas market?" I wanted to change the subject, but I wasn't ready to sleep yet. I wanted to keep talking to Della, regardless of what we were speaking about. I wanted to make up for lost time.

She smiled and nodded excitedly. "I was thinking about having Santa's Village as the theme, like the North Pole. My former assistant is sending some things over, and I'm taking a drive to Boulder tomorrow to see what I can find. I'm looking for those big, plastic candy canes, and I was thinking of a petting zoo type set-up where kids can pet some reindeers, maybe some llamas too, I'm still figuring that out, and I want a few stalls where kids can learn to make their own Christmas candy, some Christmas tree ornaments and hot chocolate with chocolate bath bombs. Maybe have a treasure hunt? I'm not sure about all the details yet." The lilt in her tone revealed her excitement, and I had to admit her idea was better than good. And it was different.

"You need to borrow the Jeep for all that? Can't imagine you'll fit much in your Lexus." I was also less worried about damage to my car.

"I'll let you know in the morning," she replied, hiding a yawn behind her hand. "What did you think about my idea for the cabin remodel?"

I quirked a brow. "You want to turn it into a luxury cabin, Della."

"Of course, I do," she laughed. "Nanna lived in that cabin her whole life, so did my mom and I. I think it's time for an upgrade, don't you?"

I chuckled. "Sure, but once everyone sees it, they'll want theirs remodeled too, and you know it's just me and Kyle."

"Would it hurt getting some help? Wouldn't be a bad thing to expand your own business, you know. Besides, it'd be good for tourism if Kipsty became known for luxury cabins. Like yours but on a smaller scale."

"You have a good point." It was my turn to yawn.

"We should get some sleep," Della murmured. She moved to get up, but I pulled her back by her arm.

"Where are you going?"

"Uh..." she blinked, "...to my room?"

I shook my head. "Not happening, Della Marie." I chuckled when she gave me *the* look. She hated being called Della Marie, and I knew it. "You're staying right here, where you've always belonged." I tucked her close to my side again and grabbed the duvet we'd kicked off at some point. I covered us both, made sure she was comfortable, and tucked my nose in her hair.

It didn't take long for her breathing to even out first, and for a while, all I did was listen to the steady cadence of her breath. I looked and saw her lashes fanned across her cheeks, remembering just how many times we'd fallen asleep like this. A small part of me was worried she'd get tired of Kipsty and leave again, but something about her seemed far more settled now than the day she left.

Something in me felt more settled too, and perhaps it was the knowledge that it wasn't me who wasn't enough. Della left because she felt stuck in a small town and needed to experience the world. And I came to the realization that I had expected her to just wait for me when I knew she wanted out. College wasn't something she wanted either, and at the time, I was happy to go to class Monday through Friday and come home for the weekend. But *I* was happy, and at the time, I'd failed to see that Della wasn't. So instead of supporting her the way I should have, I took it personally.

Maybe if I'd supported her the way I could have, she could have left, and we'd have made it work somehow. But I couldn't see anything past my own life then, and I assumed Della would always be there. What I knew now at 30 that I didn't know then was that the first time Della left, I had it in me to just let things be instead of trying to manipulate the situation to suit my needs at the expense of Della's.

A kernel of hope nudged its way into my chest, and I felt grounded in the knowledge that Della wasn't going to leave again. I believed her when she said she wasn't going anywhere. I couldn't ignore the way we'd gravitated towards each other as soon as she arrived, though, and when I looked at her, even now, my heart beat out the word *home*. Because Della *was* my home, and I'd just been waiting for her to come back. Even if I didn't know it, my heart did.

I rolled over, giving the big, fat moon and the floor-to-ceiling windows my back, and slid my hand around Della's waist to push her deeper into my chest and tangle our legs together. And if I had it my way, we'd stay like that. My mind flashed forward in time, a vision just like this playing out, and I liked what I saw.

Chapter 11

Della

Three weeks later

I stumbled through Greer's front door, arms laden with brown paper bags from the Christmas market. It had been one of the most successful markets the town had had in years, and I was damn proud to have pulled it off. Though, if I was honest, I'd pulled off bigger events under more pressure and in less time, too, so a Christmas Market in three weeks was nothing to me.

I may have sold my business and quit the industry, but I still thrived under pressure and made it work. Greer appeared at the top of the staircase and walked down, helping me take the bags to the kitchen. He peered into a few and shook his head.

"You didn't tell me you were a shopaholic," he teased, his mouth tilted to one side. I blew an errant strand of hair from my face, and smiled.

"I couldn't help myself. They had some really nice things on sale this year, and I figured we could use some new decorations for our Christmas tree. Had to get the good stuff on day one." A tree Greer hadn't put up since he divorced Maisy. I'd put it up the day before, and after my little shopping spree today, I'd have wrapped gifts surrounding the tree in no time.

I walked over to Greer, and wrapped my arms around his waist, looking up at him. "How did you and Kyle get on with the cabin today?"

After that first night with Greer, we had a lengthy chat about Nanna's cabin, and what I really wanted to do with it. Greer nixed my idea to move in there, and insisted I just stay with him. On the other hand, I didn't want to let the cabin go so we've spoken about renting it out. And as expected, as soon as people in town started noticing the updated renovations, they started asking Greer and Kyle to renovate their cabins too. Greer was in the process of hiring more hands, but that meant getting people from the next town over. He didn't have much of a choice, though. His business was growing, and he'd have to grow with it to keep up. It was all a series of *fortunate* events, I guess, since I arrived, and I couldn't be more pleased. And I hadn't felt more settled in years.

"Got a lot done, actually," he replied, locking his hands in the hollow of my back. "We should be done in a few weeks, and then we'll start on the next one." I stretched onto the balls of my feet and kissed him. "That's good news. Daisy-May is beside herself with all the patrons at the diner because the Christmas Market started so well today and will be so successful, so I guess that's another win."

Greer hummed and lowered his head, brushing his lips across mine. "Missed you today." We'd been inseparable, for the most part, since the first night I slept in his bed, and rather than feel panicky about it, like I thought I would, I felt calm, and completely at ease with how everything was turning out between us. I tried imagining a different outcome, but every one included Greer, and this was by far my favorite.

There was no talk of me leaving again, and that seemed to negate any worries either of us might've had on the subject. We were in a good place, and I soaked it like a sponge.

"Missed you more," I replied against his mouth. His eyes were ablaze with desire and delirium, and I was sure my eyes reflected the same.

"Have you eaten?" he asked, brushing my hair from my face and removing my beanie and my scarf.

"Grabbed something at the market," I told him. I had a feeling I knew where he was going with this, and I liked it. "You?"

"Grabbed something with Kyle at the diner," he replied. "Told him I had plans tonight."

I quirked a brow. "Plans?"

"Plans," he repeated before sealing his mouth over mine. Oh, so it was *those* kinds of plans.

I giggled against his mouth and pulled away. "You had me this morning," I teased, though I wasn't about to deny him a damn thing right now.

He grinned, showing off his straight white teeth. "And I'm about to have you again. I've got a decade worth of time to make up for." This time, when he kissed me, we didn't pull away. He lifted me with ease, and while he devoured my mouth and I devoured his, he carried me upstairs to our room. Things had happened so fast, but part of me wondered if the universe was just waiting for me to come back so it could all finally fall into place the way it should have.

I stripped out of my parka and lifted my long-sleeve Henley over my head. I shook my hair out and went back to kissing Greer. He dropped me on the bed, making me laugh, and I watched with greed as he removed his shirt and his jeans. I pushed my jeans down my legs and giggled when Greer grabbed a leg and haphazardly flung it over his shoulder. He watched as I got rid of my panties and my bra and then removed his boxer briefs before grabbing a condom from his bedside table. I sat, and as soon as he crawled onto the bed, and laid on his back, I straddled his hips and slid the condom on.

We'd had sex in many positions, and often too, but this was probably my favorite. On my knees, I took his hard shaft in my hand and pushed the head through the lips of my sex, shivering when I applied a bit of pressure over my clit and at my entrance.

Greer gripped my hips and murmured, "Go slow." But I had

other plans in mind. I toyed with myself a little, hearing Greer breathe out heavily while his eyes tracked my movements. I'd very quickly learned he liked watching his cock fill me, like watching my body taking him in. I swallowed and blew out a harsh breath before dropping down until he was buried to the hilt.

"Christ," he cursed, gripping my hips hard enough that he was sure to leave marks. Not that I minded. I leaned my body forward, pressing my lips to Greer's while my fingers dove into his hair. I teased him with my tongue, felt his hands slide around to my butt, and then I sat up, leaning my hands on his thighs. Ever so methodically, I lifted my hips, giving him a front-row seat to the view of him sliding in and out, in and out. He gritted his teeth, a muscle popping in his jaw as a growl surfaced from deep in his chest.

I knew he liked it, but I also knew I'd drive us both insane if I didn't pick up the pace. I threw my head back and bit my lip, sniffling a whimper. It was a true testament to my patience, and Greer's determination, because seconds later, I sat upright and held onto Greer's forearms while he started lifting me up and down.

I fell forward, resting my hands on his chest, and started moving faster. The room filled with the sound of skin-to-skin contact, my whimpers, his grunts and it made for an erotic, if not lewd, symphony. Without warning, Greer flipped us, and started thrusting in earnest.

"Oh God," I cried, my hands slipping over his damp skin. "Harder. Greer." I swallowed, and let out a mewl, feeling the heat start to pool low in my belly. It was my turn to lick my lips and grit my teeth because the bang of the headboard joined the symphony of our chaos.

Breathing hard and fast, Greer sucked my lip into his mouth, and bit. The way he took me and the way I gave myself to him was so feral.

Hearts pounding, bodies colliding, I gave him a wide-eyed look to warn him I was close.

"Greer," I whispered, begging for him to get me there. I was desperate to crash over that cliff, but like always, I wanted him there with me. His eyes were crazed, and when he thrust harder but slower, I knew he was chasing the flames that would incinerate us both alive soon enough.

I lifted a trembling hand, and gripped his nape, digging my nails into his flesh. I held on to him like that when we finally lit up like a wildfire and flew over that delicious and decadent cliff, shaking and quivering helplessly until we floated down.

His hot breath fanned the skin on my neck, and I could feel his pulse dancing as erratically as my own.

When he'd somewhat slowed his breathing, he lowered himself on top of me, still buried between my legs, and I parted my thighs to make room for his waist. He wiped my sweaty forehead and gave me a sex-lazy smile.

"Gets better every time, doesn't it?"

I smiled because he was right. Every time with him felt new and exciting. "I hope it never changes."

A while later, after we'd showered and made something to eat, we sat on the sofa, my head on his lap, watching the snow outside the large floor-to-ceiling windows.

"Do you believe in fate?" he asked, his voice low. I looked up and found he was watching me.

"Sometimes," I replied. "But I also believe we make our own fate. Losing your parents wasn't fate, and having my mother drop me on Nanna's porch before leaving for good wasn't fate, but those things haven't defined us." His hand rested on my chest, and I threaded our fingers together. "But I believe I was meant to come back," I added quietly. "In my own time, I guess."

"Did you think about me when you decided to come back?" His voice was low but laced with curiosity.

I nibbled the side of my mouth, deliberating how much to tell him. Eventually, I decided to just be honest.

"Every day between the time I left New York to when I got to Kipsty," I admitted on an exhale. "I was terrified you'd be married and have kids because I'd always thought that was *our* future, you know? I mean, we were young when we were together, but even then, my future, every which way I looked at it, included you. It's why leaving you tore me up inside. It felt as though I was sacrificing the love of my life to live a life I fell in love with, and that didn't even feel fair. So, of course, I wondered about you over the years. Every time I called Nanna, I had to stop myself from asking about you in case you'd moved on. I wanted you to be happy, but..." I shook my head a little, "...I struggled with the idea of you loving someone else the way you loved me. And I knew I'd never love someone the way I loved you. It was impossible, Greer. I resigned myself to the fact that I'd have to *settle* because I'd left most of my heart here with you."

I blew out a breath, and only then realized I had tears pooling in my eyes. I looked away, but Greer shifted so he could settle me on his lap. His strong, capable hands cupped my cheeks, his thumbs wiping the tears sliding down my face. "I don't regret leaving," I told him. "I needed to grow and find my own way, but you were never far." I lifted his hand and placed it over my heart. "I carried you with me for eleven years."

I sucked in a breath and waited, tracing Greer's masculine features with my eyes. He was beautiful and so divine. I saw my whole life flashing in his eyes, and that made my heart flutter in the confines of my ribcage.

He swallowed audibly, breathing out through his nose when he replied, "I tried falling in love again, Della." The admission stung, but I had no right to feel jealous, so I did my best to quash the feeling in my chest. "But no one ever came close to you. I chose you when I was sixteen. I just didn't realize back then it was for keeps. And I didn't think you'd ever come back..." he trailed off, and it felt as though I could read his mind. He was scared I'd never come back but also tried hard to move on, only to be left disappointed when the me-shaped hole in his heart wouldn't fit anyone else. Little did he know, it was the same for me.

"I never stopped loving you, Greer," I shivered, my voice trembling. "I still do, and it scares me because it was so all-consuming the first time, and now it feels so much bigger."

"Because it is." He rested his forehead against mine. "I never stopped loving you either. I didn't know how so I just stopped trying."

I held onto his wrists, brushing the underside with my thumbs. "How about now?" I asked. "We can't go back in time, but maybe we can start again?" I wanted that, more than he knew. And then he smiled.

"I started again the moment I saw you standing in Nanna's cabin, looking a little lost, and I wanted nothing more than to find you again."

I sighed, the sound a burst of relief and pure affection for this man. "I'm glad you found me," I whispered. "I didn't realize it, but I was waiting for you to find me."

Epilogue

Greer

One year later

I never imagined what my wedding day would look like, just that it would be Della meeting me at the altar; Maisy and I had had a court wedding, and looking back now, I had been adamant about that. I watched her careful steps as Kyle escorted her down the aisle and closer to me. The small church was filled to capacity with our friends and loved ones sitting in the rows of pews.

The officiant smiled down at me and then looked at Kyle. "Who gives this woman away?"

"I do," Kyle replied, reaching for my hand to shake. Della and I spoke about this part at length when we started planning our wedding, and it seemed fitting to have Kyle give her away. He'd never admit to anyone that he got teary-eyed the day we asked him, but he did. He kissed Della on the cheek and helped her up the steps until she faced me. She took my breath away, her white gown flowing around her on the floor. Her shoulders were bare, her blonde hair falling around her in curls. Her blue eyes shined, and her smile was happy.

Once Kyle took his seat, I took Della's hands in mine and felt them tremble. Or maybe it was my hands that were trembling.

"Friends, family, loved ones..." the officiant started, "...we are gathered here today to celebrate the love between Della and Greer and the life they will share together." He made a speech about forever and love, but I was only half-listening. I was too busy staring at Della to pay much attention. Until he cleared his throat. I blinked and looked at him.

"Pardon?" I asked, feeling my cheeks warm when my question caused our guests to laugh.

"Your vows," the officiant said. "Must I repeat them?"

I grinned, and Della giggled. "Please."

He smiled. "Do you Greer, take this woman to be your lawfully wedded wife, to live together in matrimony, to love her, comfort her, honor and keep her, in sickness and in health, in sorrow and in joy, to have and to hold from this day forward, as long as you both shall live?"

I licked my lips, still smiling. "I do."

He looked at Della.

"Do you, Della, take this man to be your lawfully wedded husband, to live together in matrimony, to love him, comfort him, honor and keep him, in sickness and in health, in sorrow and in joy, to have and to hold from this day forward, as long as you both shall live?"

Della's smile was iridescent. "With everything I am," she replied. "I do."

"Rings?" the officiant asked.

Kyle stood from his spot in front and handed both Della and I our rings. I held her ring over her finger.

"With this ring..." I started, "...I promise to love you with everything I am. I promise to stand by you through the hard times, the best times, and everything in between. I promise to be the best husband, the best partner, and, someday, the best father to our children. You are my beginning, my middle, and my end, and everything in between. I vow to love you until my last breath, Della. Every day, all day. Until the sun sets for the very last time." My hand shook as I slid her ring into her finger, and when I looked up, Della had tears coming down her cheeks. She held my ring over my finger and swallowed.

"With his ring..." she started, "...I promise to be your best friend, to love you every day through the good and the bad times, and whatever happens in between. I promise to cherish your heart as long as I breathe and to love you for as long as I'm alive. You are my world, my heart, my soul, my best friend and..." she licked her lips and sighed, "...the father of my child."

The church went still but only for a few seconds, long enough for me to catch what Della had said.

"What?"

She laughed and nodded, tears falling. She quietly slipped my ring on, and then I had my hands around her face. "We're pregnant?" I asked. The church filled with sound, cheers, and claps, and I pressed my mouth to Della's, feeling my heart balloon in my chest.

"We're not at this part yet," the officiant whispered, loud enough to garner some laughter from our guests. But I didn't care. I slipped my hand around Della's back, and held her to me, a vision in my head of her belly growing with our first child. God. I loved this woman more than life itself, and now we were going to have a baby, part of me and part of Della. I couldn't contain my own tears, allowing them to fall freely. I broke our kiss, and wiped Della's cheeks.

"Are you happy?" she asked quietly. I nodded, my gaze flitting between her eyes.

"Completely," I murmured, going in for another kiss, this one longer and far too inappropriate for a church. At some point, the officiant gave in and pronounced us husband and wife to another round of cheers and laughter.

Me? I was wrapped up in my *wife* and the mother of my child. Della squealed when I picked her up and swung her around, her laughter a gentle sound. I put her down and again cupped her face. "Really?" It all felt so surreal.

"Really," she replied. "I wanted to tell you this morning, before the ceremony, but..." She shrugged. "Surprise."

I laughed with pure joy and replied, "You're perfect."

"Give it a few months," she teased. "When I'm round, with swollen ankles and super cranky. Then I won't be so perfect."

I shook my head. "You'll always be perfect, Della. My kind of perfect."

~ THE END OF THE SERIES ~

If you enjoyed the *Mountain Man Daddy Series*, take a look at a sneak peek of the first book of Hadsan Cove Series: *Flames and Forget-Me-Nots.*

Prologue
Clark

Seven years ago

"Do you want to carve the turkey, Clark?" Dad asked me in a vain attempt to drown out my brother's droning through the window. I was craning my neck to see them on the porch. Poor Isla looked devastated. I could see her trembling, although it was cold, and neither of them had worn their jackets.

"Brady said he wanted to do it," I said flatly.

"I don't think he's coming back," Dad said pointedly. He even held out the carving knife across the table for me to take.

Brady caused some drama like this every holiday season. He was always the center of attention, always ready to put on a morbid Christmas show against our will. It was even snowing this year, and it would've been romantic if he was trying to patch things up. We couldn't keep letting him get away with it.

"It'll get cold," my mother added hopefully, but I had lost interest in the meal already. It was always better warmed up the next day, anyway.

To make matters worse, the next song on the playlist started, and I heard Paul Young crooning the opening lines of "Do They Know It's Christmas?" Evidently, they did not.

That was enough for me, and to the tuts of my parents, I left the dining table and crept over to the front door, where I could see their silhouettes clearly through the fogged glass. Their voices were much clearer now.

"You still haven't explained to me why you keep going back to Mary-Anne," Isla said to Brady with a sigh. Even through the glass,

I could see her stiffen, and her voice became sharper.

"I don't know."

"When was the last time?"

"November."

"Just the once?"

"Twice."

"Can't you see she just wants to use you? She never loved you. You were always her backup plan."

This made Brady scowl. It was a fair comment.

"There's no need to be mean," he whined.

"Mean?! You've just admitted to cheating on me, again, with Mary-Anne, again, and you think what I said to you is mean?"

"Yes, you always do this." Brady huffed.

"I always do this? You slept with her last Christmas, right when we started seeing each other. You said our relationship was new and didn't think it would last. You said you came clean about it because you wanted to take things seriously."

"Look, Isla, can we not make a scene? You did this last year, too. We're supposed to be having Christmas dinner with my family."

"Why did you bring it up then?"

"OK. Alright. I'm sorry I mentioned it. Are you happy now?"

"No! And you can try to pretend you mean it. You always sound so cavalier. Why would you do this at your parents' house? Am I supposed to go back there now and pretend everything is fine?"

"If that's what you want to do, but I'd rather you just take off to save me the trouble of having to get through the evening with you," Brady said, venom in his tone, just as Simon Le Bon sang 'There's a world outside your window, and it's a world of dread and fear.'

That was enough for me. I grabbed their coats on the coat rack by the front door, opened the door, and the sound of the latch was enough to burst their bubble. Both of them were immediately silent when I stepped out onto the porch, like I was a schoolteacher catching two of my pupils being mischievous. They both crossed their arms, and before Isla turned away from me, I saw the tears welling in her eyes.

"It's freezing outside. Bundle up," I said, looking between them as I handed them their coats. Isla took hers without looking at me, while Brady practically snatched his, giving an ungrateful scoff. Any other time, I would have torn him a new one for being disrespectful, but the look on Isla's face had been enough to mellow me out.

I heard Isla stifling a sniffle. Poor girl. She deserved better than Brady. I don't know why she kept going back to him. She could do so much better, and could have been with any number of guys who wouldn't have done what he did so callously, so remorselessly. There really was no need for her to keep going through this song and dance over and over.

She was right, too: he wasn't really sorry. He still preferred Mary-Anne, and he always had. They'd been high school sweethearts, though if you ask me, there was nothing sweet about their relationship. Brady had always been wrapped around her little finger, and for the life of me, I couldn't understand how he didn't see right through her. So when Mary-Anne broke up with Brady on their high school graduation day, he'd been devastated. In fact, I'm sure he only started seeing Isla initially to see if it would make her jealous enough to take him back, but when it didn't work, he was stuck with Isla. Whenever Mary-Anne came calling, he would go running back, and I was sure she often did so only to see if he still would.

"Let's take a walk, Brady," I said curtly to him, tapping him on the shoulder and nodding at the driveway.

"Alright. Seeing as it looks like I won't be staying anymore, I will need a hotel, anyway. I parked at the bottom of the hill 'cause of the ice. You can walk me to my car."

"Alright, just hang on one second," I told him, then showed Isla inside. Isla gave Brady a forlorn look before walking through the door frame. But Brady pulled at his coat impatiently, puffing out cold breath. He rubbed his hands, looking towards the bottom of the hill.

Annoyance boiled in me. I'd be having words with him on our way down.

"Is she alright, Clark?" Mom asked.

"Yes, she's fine. I'm just going to sit with her in the living room. I'll come back in a minute."

I took Isla into the living room next to the dining room. It was cozy, with a shag carpet and newly polished wooden furnishings. It was small, but big enough for the two of us to fit inside comfortably. There was a fireplace and a small couch. She walked straight over to the couch and lay down, facing away from me. She was still cradling herself.

"Do you want me to carve you some turkey? I can bring your plate in here for you," I asked her as I took a blanket out from a nearby basket where my mother liked to pack away extra blankets and pillows, and shook it out for her.

She didn't respond. I felt awful for her. She was curled up in the fetal position, wiping her face with her hands. I threw the blanket over her and tucked her in.

"Thank you," she whispered.

"Do you want the fire on?"

"Yes, please," squeaked the reply. I got on my knees at the fireplace and threw a log in. I hadn't done this in years and almost forgot to add a firestarter, which was in one of the drawers of the console table next to the couch. I felt her eyes on me as I passed her, then searched frantically through each drawer from top to bottom. My heart raced when I saw her watching me through my periphery. I couldn't believe the power she had over me, even in the vulnerable state she was in.

I remembered last Christmas when Brady had done the same thing to her. She'd been dismayed. I couldn't believe, after all that, he had the gall to do it all over again.

Once I got the fire going after what felt like an age, I returned to her, proud of myself.

"Thank you," she whispered, settling down now as the tears started to subside. As I looked down at her amid the flickering flames, I could see her face was still wet. I subconsciously stroked her hair, which calmed her even more and then leaned towards her to kiss her on the forehead.

But as I did so, she turned towards me and reached out, catching my cheek as our noses were close to touching. I froze, unsure of what to do or what she thought as she looked up at me. Her damp eyes sparkled in the firelight, and her dark hair was sprawled out over the couch like an inviting blanket. I noticed a tiny mole on her lower cheek, which made her look like Marilyn Monroe.

It felt so intimate being that close. The crackling of the wood behind me sounded like whatever was being ignited within me by her touch and in receiving her gaze. It washed over us with its warmth.

I had tried to suppress it for so long, ever since she'd started seeing Brady, but my heart was racing now. She placed her other palm on my chest with such a delicate curiosity. She could feel my heart reaching a crescendo, anticipating something forbidden happening between us, and there was no hiding it. There was only the unspoken truth.

She looked at my chest, and back at me. She didn't recoil or protest. She was waiting for what I was going to do next. Welcoming it, even.

I wondered how she would taste if I kissed her now, and how her damp, excited tongue would feel running over mine. Her perfume was so sweet, it was intoxicating, and now all I could think about was feeling her pressed against me with her legs wrapped tightly around my waist.

I was so close. It would be so easy, but the door leading to the hallway was still ajar, just barely out of my reach. My brother was waiting for me outside. My parents could hear from the dining room.

Isla was stunningly beautiful, and she had changed so much in the last year or so since she'd gotten together with Brady. She had just turned eighteen then, both of them in the first year of college a town over from Hadsan Cove. She had much more confidence now. Her touch was so pure as I felt the firm tip of her fingernail on my temple, and her thumb under my chin. She was guiding me to her, and I was utterly powerless to stop her as I hungered for her. I felt that nonexistent gap between us shrinking as she exhaled, and I breathed in her breath that beckoned me to the source just as Band Aid started to sing 'feed the woooorld' next door in their final climax.

Will Isla and Clark find their way back to each other? What happens when a blast from the past returns wanting to make amends? Will Clark prove to Isla that he is the man for her? Will Isla finally put herself first?

Book 1 is now available!

Printed in Great Britain
by Amazon

19366795R00058